LEW GRADE AND CARLO PONTI PRESENT
FOR ASSOCIATED GENERAL FILMS
AN INTERNATIONAL CINE PRODUCTIONS FILM

SOPHIA LOREN   RICHARD HARRIS

MARTIN SHEEN   O. J. SIMPSON
LIONEL STANDER   ANN TURKEL

with
INGRID THULIN
and

LEE STRASBERG

and BURT LANCASTER   and AVA GARDNER
as MACKENZIE   as NICOLE
in

THE CASSANDRA CROSSING

starring
LOU CASTEL   TOM HUNTER   JOHN PHILIP LAW   RAY LOVELOCK
ALIDA VALLI

MUSIC BY JERRY GOLDSMITH

SCREENPLAY BY
TOM MANKIEWICZ and ROBERT KATZ & GEORGE PAN COSMATOS

STORY BY ROBERT KATZ and GEORGE PAN COSMATOS

PANAVISION®   TECHNICOLOR®

PRODUCED BY CARLO PONTI

DIRECTED BY GEORGE PAN COSMATOS

RELEASED I

D1388227

The Cassandra Crossing

a novelization by Robert Katz

based on the screenplay by
Tom Mankiewicz, Robert Katz and George Pan Cosmatos

Pan Original
Pan Books London and Sydney

First published 1977 by Pan Books Ltd,
Cavaye Place, London sw10 9pg
© Robert Katz and George Pan Cosmatos 1977
isbn 0 330 24397 7
Printed and bound in Great Britain by
Richard Clay (The Chaucer Press) Ltd, Bungay, Suffolk

To Peter Matson

THE TRANSCONTINENTAL EXPRESS

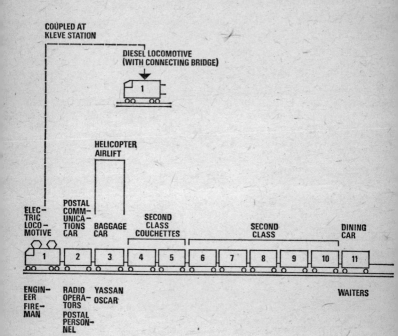

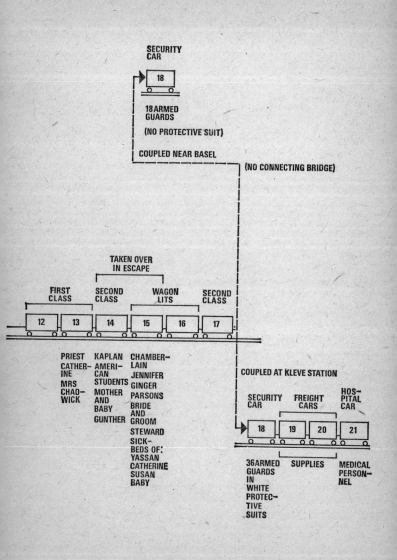

SECURITY CAR

18

18 ARMED GUARDS

(NO PROTECTIVE SUIT)

COUPLED NEAR BASEL

(NO CONNECTING BRIDGE)

TAKEN OVER IN ESCAPE

FIRST CLASS | SECOND CLASS | WAGON LITS | SECOND CLASS

12 | 13 | 14 | 15 | 16 | 17

PRIEST
CATHERINE
MRS CHADWICK

KAPLAN
AMERICAN STUDENTS
MOTHER AND BABY
GUNTHER

CHAMBERLAIN
JENNIFER
GINGER
PARSONS
BRIDE AND GROOM
STEWARD
SICK-BEDS OF:
YASSAN
CATHERINE
SUSAN
BABY

COUPLED AT KLEVE STATION

SECURITY CAR | **FREIGHT CARS** | **HOSPITAL CAR**

18 | 19 | 20 | 21

36 ARMED GUARDS IN WHITE PROTECTIVE SUITS

SUPPLIES

MEDICAL PERSONNEL

Author's note

Within the limits of the narrative powers of the writer, the events recounted in these pages are true. I have met, known, or have come to know, in varying degrees of intimacy, many of the persons whose story is told here. I have followed the iron trail of the Transcontinental Express to an unfriendly sky at the old Cassandra Crossing. I have, with the kind assistance of someone who must remain anonymous, examined the classified 'Milestone' papers, and with the aid of spectrum analysers, computers, graphical displays and other sophisticated instruments, I have been able to retrieve an invaluable, twenty-eight-hour and twenty-three-minute tape recording believed to have been obliterated.

I doubt that many readers will recall the news involving the Transcontinental Express, train number 5072, though it occurred only months ago. In the first place, it was inaccurately reported – to say the least – and in the second, coverage was far from extensive. We now know that in both instances this was deliberate, not as much on the part of the media as on the authorities, who, for reasons which I hope to make clear and which some undoubtedly will judge to be more or less valid, undertook a concerted effort to cover up the facts.

I have before me photocopies of the incomplete Associated Press and Reuter files on the original story. It was the AP who broke the 'news' with the following dispatch, reproduced in its entirety:

OSTRAVA, Czechoslovakia, 13 March (AP)
A twenty-seven-year-old shepherd showed up at police headquarters this afternoon claiming to have seen a 'gigantic' passenger train crossing the High Tatra range of the Carpathian Mountains and headed towards the Polish border, nineteen miles north-east of here.

The shepherd, Jan Cieszyn, who gave his residence as 'in the mountains', said the train bore the name 'Transcontinental Express' and the number '5072'.

'I saw hundreds of people on board,' Mr Cieszyn declared, 'and everyone seemed to be staring out the windows hypnotically. Among them were men in white suits wearing white hoods. I think they were armed.'

Following a brief investigation, authorities later characterized the alleged sighting as being 'highly unlikely'. They pointed out that the Transcontinental Express – train number 5072 – was on a run between Geneva and Stockholm, through Western Europe, and could not have come within five hundred rail miles of here. They also noted that there had been festivals in several local villages last night and that the hard-drinking mountain shepherds are traditionally tellers of tall tales.

Authorities did not explain, however, how Mr Cieszyn knew the name and precise number of the train.

Reuters had little to add, and all the subsequent dispatches which appeared over the next three or four days are ambiguous and generally unenlightening. Walter Cronkite, in a brief summary telecast on the 17th (recorded the previous day, however), linked the story to intriguing but unconfirmed reports from European police sources of a 'wave' of missing persons. He asked a pointed question: 'If not in the Carpathians, where is the Transcontinental Express?' There, with no answer forthcoming, international 'coverage' died, and presumably was forgotten. Who can remember yesterday's inside pages?

But the story of the Transcontinental Express, which crossed into Poland 13 March last carrying more than 1,200 men, women and children (the majority of them West Europeans, Britons and Americans) merits recall. For the train, the passengers, and the crew, as far as is publicly known, vanished.

I first met the man who sent the Transcontinental Express on its singular journey to Poland, a Canadian scientist named Stephen Mackenzie, early in 1964. I had just completed an assignment in the press department of the United Nations in New York; at the time I thought I was temporarily between jobs, since I expected to be taken on as a press officer at the first United Nations Conference on Trade and Development, which I believe was scheduled to open in Geneva in February or March of that year. My family and I had come to Europe that particularly cold winter and we were living in a small hotel in Rome awaiting word to take up the post, which had been promised to me in an unofficial way. As it turned out, I never got the job, nor, for that matter, any other job since then, for after I met Mackenzie one thing led to another and I ended up in the erratic business of freelance writing, a rather reckless occupation for a man with a wife and two sons to look after.

In Rome, while waiting for that call that never came, I ran into Jennifer Saint, a most remarkable woman whose acquaintance the reader – if not already familiar with her work and reputation as one of the world's most original photo-journalists – will make in some detail in these pages. Jennifer had won a *Prix de Rome* in photography and was at the ivory-tower-like American Academy in the green part of town, taking a year off from the freelance chase (she was to spend the next five or six years dodging anti-personnel weapons, defoliants and search-and-destroy assaults in Vietnam). Jennifer helped keep our family in bread, wine and rent that year, supplying me with story leads, and one of them led to a *Playboy* interview I did with Mackenzie.

The sixties, at least part of the decade, was an all-too-brief golden 'aglet' in magazine journalism and I was paid an exhilarating fee, though the piece was never used. The reason was, as far as I can surmise from what Hefner told me the only time I ever met him (in an elevator in Chicago's Merchandise Mart), that the interview had suddenly been deprived of its topicality when Mackenzie was moved out of

the job he was holding at the time: an expert in bacteriological warfare. I didn't agree. But I knew something I'd
purposely left out of my story, respecting Mackenzie's re-
quest.

The interview had been conducted in the old NATO headquarters in Paris. I found Mackenzie to be in possession of
one of those superminds that makes your own head feel like
it's stuffed with old socks, and he had the kind of cutting
wit that could slice smoked salmon. He was also filling me
with a paddock full of PR horseshit and at a certain point I
stood up, switched off my ancient, eighteen-pound Wollen-
sak, and said, 'Sir, I think germ warfare is the greatest thing
mankind ever invented since toilet paper and I have not the
slightest doubt that when this interview is published the
entire free world will agree.' He laughed, chortled. Then we
went to lunch at Lucas Carton, near the Opera, and over a
bottle of Château Lagrange, to some extent he opened up.

Stephen 'Duke' Mackenzie was one of those men who believed in working for the Good Cause 'within the system', as
the saying goes. A writer meets a lot of them in the capital
cities of the world; a reader gets to know them in many
books. Among Hitler's generals and diplomats self-styled
doves were legion and once there was a war to end all wars.
But Mackenzie represented somewhat of a difference, I sup-
pose. He told me that afternoon that he had one aim only:
to work himself and everyone around him out of a job. He
succeeded. My interview lost its 'topicality', but NATO phased
out germ warfare, as did the NATO countries, notably the US.*
Moreover a great many bacteriological warriors found themselves suddenly unemployed. Mackenzie went to work for
the UN in Geneva – in the field of public health. A within-
the-system triumph? Perhaps. But look at it this way. In

* For an assessment of Mackenzie's influence on governmental poli-
cies in this connection, see Colonel H. A. Eberhardt, *The Military
Value of CBW* (Washington: Government Printing Office, 1970)

Geneva, Mackenzie got to head up 'Milestone', a top secret UN operation (now disbanded) which was supposed to protect the lives of millions but in the end was the bane of the Transcontinental Express.

In any event, Duke Mackenzie lays no claims to any victories and he no longer operates within. Ask him now, and he'll tell you that the bacteriological warfare programmes were doomed without him by their own internal logic, and, as will be seen from what follows, even in Milestone's most critical hour, when Mackenzie appeared to hold in his hands alone a power more awesome than that of any king or president, he never lost sight of the illusory nature of such control.

Today Mackenzie lives in early retirement. He'll be fifty-four this year. His style is modest, rural, far from the centres of the powers once at his command. He has read these pages. Indeed he has contributed much to the reconstruction I've attempted here. For whatever worth may in the end be attributed to it he has authorized me to state on his behalf, 'It is good that the whole truth be known.'

A word remains to be said about Jonathan Chamberlain, the man who for a span of hours that must have seemed like a long forever found himself at impossible odds with Mackenzie – though the two were never to stand face to face. It is difficult to know Chamberlain. On the day he boarded the Transcontinental Express, which was the day he met and was taken with Jennifer Saint, he was a surgeon at the pinnacle of what is generally called a brilliant career. He had long been associated with Harvard Medical School, and a search through the *New York Times* 'Index' shows his name connected with attending this or that celebrity, this or that statesman or other well-known name. By his own admission more a craftsman than a man of science, he can be found in the arena of controversy only once, it appears, when in 1969 and 1970 he spoke out forcefully against the heart transplanters. A big New Mexican, he was born in 1932 in Placitas, an old Indian settlement just north of Albuquerque, which seems to have given him those qualities of reserve, economy of movement and good-scoutism rather common among those who wax on the thin air of high plateaux. The strong, silent type, I guess you'd say. Oddly, a lot like Stephen Mackenzie.

Yet theirs was a clash of opposites, a conflict between science and more ancient wisdom, between a faceless society's belief in numbers and a dwindling breed of man which still believes in people.

*

This book could not have been written without the help and encouragement of a great many people, to all of whom I am deeply grateful. To protect the identities of some of them, I have not made annotated references to my sources, believing, in any event, that most are more or less apparent from the internal evidence. In the few cases where they are not, and the still fewer where it may seem that it would not have been possible to have acquired the information reported, or, on the other hand, that some minor, though perhaps curiosity-satisfying, intimate details are being withheld, I beg the reader's indulgence in my commitment to honour the wishes of certain private parties.

Finally, I would like to record my specific thanks to the following persons: George Pan Cosmatos, whose contribution was as inestimable as it was personally inspiring; his wife, Birgitta; and my own wife, Beverly; as well as Carlo Ponti, Phil Feldman and Martin Erlichman.

R.K.
Rome, Italy

Friday

noon to midnight

1 noon

'Do you speak English?'

The voice was muffled, though insistent, urgent, for an old man lay dying in a bed.

'Parla italiano? ... Deutsch? Sprechen sie Deutsch?'

The old man opened his mouth. His tongue was swollen, covered with a yellowish coating, thick, furry, like the quivering body of the velvet ant. He groaned, uselessly.

'Where was he going? You must tell us!'

Mackenzie heard and watched. He stood at a panel of tinted glass which looked on to the underground isolation chamber. A windowless, stark white room. No furniture, only the spartan death bed. Three figures in white dressed in overalls, elbow-length gloves, slitted hoods, goggles, and plastic deflection masks – a sort of beak giving them an eagle-like appearance.

They hovered over the old man, who seemed a kind of fallen marionette suspended from the thin tubes carrying plasma to his veins.

'You have got to try!'

The reels of a Uhrer 5000 turned beneath Mackenzie's fingertips. The machine had been fitted with a red control which bore the word, 'Destruct'. But now, inside the isolation room, a microphone hung close to the velvet ant recording every ugly sound.

'Yhhnnehh...'

Mackenzie, watching the feeble heart-scrawl on the oscilloscope inside, knew the old man had only moments left of life. He saw his own death drift across his eyes. He knew how it felt to die, at least in the manner the old man would go: from internal asphyxiation. His head would swim for a moment or two; then he would think in whatever his language, 'I feel dizzy.' Deoxygenization of the blood would bring on giddiness, a high, a slowly lowering curtain of unconsciousness, not an all-unpleasant passage to eternity.

The old man's lips were blue. They parted. With great effort, he raised his head from his pillow and spoke, uttering low, guttural sounds. They resembled words. Unintelligible words. His head fell back. The cathode ray formed an unbroken line on the green screen. His eyes remained open, devoid of the corneal reflex. He was dead.

The three ghostly figures turned to the plate glass, a question in their faceless posture. Mackenzie, before he stopped the tape, touched a switch which allowed him to speak to the men inside. His tense words were recorded, though we have only our knowledge of the man to recover his grim sentiments.

'Burn him,' he said.

*

The Hôpital Jean Jacques Fazy in the Quai du Président Wilson on the North Shore of Lake Geneva was built in 1897 with funds from the de Saussure family. Philanthropic, Swiss, and above all Calvinist, they had had the thrifty idea of commemorating the fiftieth anniversary of the fruit of Fazy's little revolution – a liberal constitution – and for the same money, the one hundred and tenth anniversary of Horace Bénédict de Saussure's conquest of Mont Blanc.

The isolation complex was installed in the basement of the hospital in 1973 by the United Nations at a money's-no-object cost far greater than that of erecting the entire building, but doubtless the de Saussures and even Calvin himself would have approved. A floating structure enclosed in an envelope of plastic and steel, the chamber, with an interior outdoing any Kubrikian mission control, celebrates economy of time and motion. Moreover it commemorates, as it were, Carl Langer's and Max Bernstein's not-so-little revolution in ecological epidemiology, the fruit of which was the Milestone project, with its ambitious (if not pretentious), and, as it turned out, disastrous aim of saving in spite of itself all of the human race.

*

Mackenzie leaned over the tape recorder, playing and re-playing the old man's dying words. Elena Lindstrom listened with him.

'Arabic,' she said. She knew the language intimately. As a scientific officer of the World Health Organization, she had lived in the Sudan, Libya, and lately in the People's Republic of Yemen. For a year or so she had been married to a Libyan engineer. One night he punched her on the side of her head. She walked out, carrying behind the long golden hair that fell to her shoulders a ringing in her ear that would pursue her without respite to the grave.

'Noon train,' Elena said, translating the death words, 'to Stockholm.'

Mackenzie looked at his watch. He touched the destruct button on the tape recorder. He lifted a telephone and spoke without emotion.

'Milestone.' He hung up.

2 12.05 pm

The Transcontinental Express leaves from the Gare de Cornavin every day at noon. It goes to Basel, Paris, Brussels, Amsterdam, Copenhagen and Stockholm, with a score of intermediate stops, completing the run in twenty-nine hours and fifty-two minutes, when, as often, it fulfils timetable expectations.

The train's BSF electric engine pulls a 30,000-ton payload of sixteen cars, including dining, baggage and postal communications facilities. Of the passenger cars – consisting of six-and-a-half-foot square compartments off a lateral cor-

19

ridor thirty-nine inches wide – seven are second class, two are second-class sleepers (couchettes), two first class, and two first-class sleepers, or wagon-lits. When, on rather rare occasions, the train is full, it carries about 1,200 passengers.

On that Friday, it was full. Although there were, however, a few empty wagon-lit accommodations, second class was more than at capacity, the overflow having chosen to vie for the pullout seats in the corridors rather than pay for the princely wagon-lits. Indeed, so full was the Transcontinental Express, that it upset the conductors' routines and departed an uncustomary five minutes late.

Jennifer Saint was at that moment supposed to have been on the train. Instead, she was on the platform, running hard. Dressed in blue jeans and a tasteful collection of melodious necklaces and bracelets, she carried two small suitcases and a large leather handbag. Two Nikons swung around her long neck. She was a lithe woman, just a few weeks on the riper side of thirty at the time. Her skin glowed with the reflective power of a new leaf, and she ran with animal grace, none of that hip-churning, breast-flipflopping stuff. Her breasts bounced, to be sure, but there was tone, exquisite tone, as everyone watching her could see.

Several passengers leaned out the windows either cheering her on or simply enjoying the chase.

'Open the bloody doors!' she shouted volcanically, struggling to keep up. Her face was flushed with anger.

A group of young soldiers on board bellowed with laughter and applause.

'Up yours!' she yelled back at them.

But this only made them rowdier.

At last a door opened and the strong hand of an unseen man leaned out. She tried desperately to grab hold and finally their hands touched and locked. The man pulled her upward and she all but flew to him, causing him to lose his balance. They fell to the corridor floor, Jennifer sprawled on her back, and the man, Jonathan Chamberlain, the big New Mexican with the sharp light of the mountains in his eyes, on top.

For a moment they lay there, neither of them knowing what to do. Then Jennifer tried to get up. One of her cameras, lodged between them, was crushing her well-moulded breast.

'You're busting my lens,' she said acidly.

Chamberlain got to his feet quickly and tried to help her up, but she brushed him aside, gathered herself together, and began down the corridor towards the next car, without as much as a thanks. That's a part of Jennifer Saint. One part.

Chamberlain shrugged. Still he could not take his eyes from her. Even loaded with luggage and gear, she moved well. That's another part of Jennifer Saint.

*

By now, the Transcontinental Express raced along the right bank of Lake Geneva, de Saussure's Mont Blanc rising in the distance. The Swiss sky was limpid blue. The noonday light was mighty, yet peaceful. The train climbed for the north.

*

In one of the wagon-lit cars, a steward named Willi Tickler scurried along carrying the linens he would need for the trip. Suddenly his ears pricked. He stopped, listened for a while, then, hearing nothing, he shrugged and continued on his way.

A moment later, a pale, fragile, dark-eyed young man, with a distant, frightened look in his eyes and a strange custard colouring, slipped out of an empty compartment. He was breathing somewhat irregularly, as he moved with nervous caution, and when a conductor entered the car, he dashed back into the compartment. His name was Yassan. That morning he had brought an old man, his father, to the

Red Cross building on the Avenue de la Paix and had left him in a waiting room, where some minutes later the old man had collapsed.

Steward Tickler stored his linens and began his first real business of the day: hawking luncheon reservations. He barked in his own special way, a manner he had learned and believed he had improved upon from his predecessor.

'Lun-chin ... reservay ... shuns!' It sounded like a kind of Sino-French, and he was about to sing it again, when he came upon someone having difficulty.

'May I be of assistance, madam?'

He was talking to Jennifer Saint and he knew it, having recognized her, it seems, from photographs and television reportages he had seen, although he didn't let on.

Jennifer, still loaded down with her luggage and cameras, was searching with growing frustration for her proper place on the train. Her discomfiture was all the greater, since she regarded herself as a train buff, having acquired such rank in recent heavy-travelling years out of a positive loathing of flying, which took scant consideration of the physical and psychological limits of human biology. She was angry enough at herself for having arrived late at the station, though she pretended it her travel agent's fault, and she would have preferred to ignore the steward, but there was little more she could do than hand him her ticket.

'Is this, or isn't this first class?' she asked sharply.

'But madam is booked wagon-lit,' he replied, adding with a slight flourish of his head, 'a most elegant way to travel, for a most elegant traveller.' Undoubtedly, Steward Tickler felt he had a way with women.

Jennifer looked down at her baubles and jeans. She could feel a rivulet of perspiration running an uneconomical course to her navel. She snatched her ticket back most inelegantly, leaving hurriedly, and dragging her mule-like burdens along.

The steward was not unhurt. He took slow revenge in his own style, allowing her to go off in the wrong direction, and he felt perfectly vindicated when one of her camera straps hooked on a door handle, which caused her to stumble and brought on a sally of mumbled profanities.

Sonofabitch travel agent, she thought, knowing all the while that the wagon-lit accommodation had been her most precise instruction. She had been cherishing the idea of the forty-three square feet of solitude in her own compartment all the way to Copenhagen, particularly with someone else picking up the tab. She was on an assignment with *Fortune* to cover the Danish biennial art fair. Painting had become as beautiful as blue chips since the recent demise of the grace of the dollar, and when a Nicholson had sold for $125,000 at Sotheby's in London a few weeks back – going for three or four times what it had been valued at a year before – *Fortune* had detected a definite trend.

Jennifer liked the job. Presumably, there would be no violence (though she tried to contemplate what the terrorist international might be up to), and besides, she was a bit of a collector herself. No one who had ever had a *Prix de Rome* was not. She owned a few sculptures of Hadzi, Smyley, Suttman and Zajack, two or three of John Dowell's musical water-colours, a goblinish landscape by Gillespie (her prize possession), and all those drawings, prints and less-definable pieces Academyites acquire from each other *quid pro quo*. No Nicholsons, though.

Once she had loved a painter, a lean man who believed God was Art, and that the only way to know Him was through self-crucifixion, driving nail after nail through his own heart. Jennifer had been a nail of uncertain number, and when she had discovered this she was already several inches into the cross, which required a year of agony in the extrication. Now, however, she felt nothing, save an indefinable resentment for her travel agent. What was wrong with her today? she wondered, prophesying a lousy trip ahead.

Steward Tickler entered the next car, busy as a pinball. Chamberlain was in the corridor. The steward was having a rare beginning. Another familiar face, only this time less indirectly.

'Oh, Dr Chamberlain. Good to have you with us again.' They had met a month back on Chamberlain's last trip to Paris. The right words – they must have been right – had brought him a fifty-franc tip. 'Business or pleasure, sir?'

'A little of both ... hopefully.'

The steward knew what to say now. He had a way with men, too. He winked lasciviously.

'I should have known: Stockholm. I've quite a collection of magazines, you know.'

Chamberlain stopped him with a hand motion.

'Sorry,' he said with a polite smile, 'can't read a word of Swedish.'

Steward Tickler could not see what that had to do with it, but he felt himself plainly off base. He searched his mind for another topic of mutual interest. He was of the old school: one's tips had to be earned.

They chatted for a while, mostly about the steward's chronically ill mother, for whom he solicited Chamberlain in hope of learning the cure. Chamberlain answered with newspaper column advice and thought of Stockholm.

There would be no real business there, he was sure, and much less real pleasure. His secretary had planned the wagon-lit trip to afford him the only free time he could expect between now and his return. He was scheduled to visit the Karolinska Institute, west of Brunnsviken, to address the surgery department, attend a reception and receive an award, then on for a lightning tour of other medical schools and hospitals throughout the country. It was something one just had to do at that stage of one's career, and though he could think of no felt-reason why, he supposed that was in fact business.

Worse would follow from doing what was expected of him under what might be called the heading of pleasure. There was a certain Dr Annika Hellquist awaiting him there. She was outwardly staid, even forbidding, but not an unattractive woman. He had met her in New York several months earlier, and – through no fault or design of his own – he had had the misfortune of making the kind of personality display that brings on in predisposed cases a sloppy, one-sided infatuation as well as all the inherent, self-guilt-producing complications that invariably ensue. It had been she, he was lately convinced, who had arranged the invitation to tour and win prizes, and now, regretting the weak moment in which he had accepted, he was in for it.

Dr Hellquist, he could not doubt, would be with him every inch of the way – a ghastly phrase, he thought, since he knew from recent experience that 'every inch' would include exaggerated claims on his sexual prowess. In New York she had been capable of excessively more demands than he could ever supply, and there was no cause to hope that Stockholm would not be more of the same. And all this, he was sure, would follow midnight-sun cruises on Lake Malar and threats real or implied of a broken heart and multiple tantrums unless he complied.

Jonathan Chamberlain was not one to say no to a woman, perhaps because in his lifetime there had never been *his* woman around.

*

Joseph Kaplan, a man in his fifties on his way home to Antwerp, elbowed through a crowded corridor in a second-class car. He carried a large suitcase. Working with quiet deliberation, Kaplan set the suitcase on a pull-out seat and opened it slightly. A distinct ticking could be heard coming from the valise and it caught the ears of some passengers standing nearby, which was exactly what Kaplan wanted, for he began at once to shout to the crowd.

'Attention!' he cried. *'Achtung! ... Attenzione!'*

The crowd began to shift in Kaplan's direction, regarding him oddly. He placed his hand on the suitcase, whose contents could not be seen.

'Listen to the ticking! *... Ascoltate! ... Hören sie, zu!'*

There was a sudden silence, bewilderment, and the kind of spleen-tightening fear that came in big with the sky-jack age. Kaplan smiled devilishly.

'Tick ... tock ... tick ... tock.'

Certain he had galvanized everyone's attention, he threw open the top of the suitcase to reveal an assortment of literally hundreds of cheap watches and a store of other items, too, including cigarette lighters, transistor radios, and, not quite exposed, several gross of Korean-made condoms.

A score of spleens relaxed and the jovial enzymes flowed.

Kaplan was a travelling pedlar-salesman. He was a clownish man whose 'jolliness' could not wholly mask an immense inner burden, which he wore on the outside in two deep ruts in a cobbled face that could only have been hewed by having trafficked too long in pain. For now, he seemed merry enough, however, as he held up a tinselly, oversized watch with too many shiny dials.

'I have here,' he said, 'the world's most fascinating invention.... *Ein wahres Weltwunder habe ich hier. Ja, un miracolo!'*

Someone was edging through the crowd: Yassan.

'Now you see it,' Kaplan went on, and then – stage-magician style – he made the watch disappear. *'Voilà!* Now you don't!'

This brought a round of laughter and applause. Kaplan shuffled his watches like a cardsharp. A ray of light caromed from the casings, striking Yassan's eyes. His hand went up as a shield. He was sweating, trembling, and he had begun to cough persistently.

A conductor entered the compartment. Kaplan quickly closed up shop. Yassan wheeled around and staggered off.

*

Chamberlain was about to return to his compartment when he caught sight of Jennifer. She had found her error and was now busily checking the letters and numbers on the compartment doorposts. Chamberlain pointed to the one next to his.

'All yours ... Jennifer Saint.'

A 'how-did-you-know' look flashed across Jennifer's face, but a moment later she was as prohibitive as ever. She examined the markings on the compartment and began moving in.

'Don't you want to know how I know so much?' Chamberlain asked, watching her without offering a helping hand.

'I'll bet you'll tell me,' she said wryly, unburdening herself of her gear and paying scarce attention to him.

'The steward. Your fan. Reads everything you write ... Seems he collects all kinds of magazines.'

Chamberlain picked up a copy of *Newsweek* lying among her things, flipping through the pages distractedly while speaking.

'He says *everybody* loves you.'

Chamberlain found a picture of Jennifer interviewing a silver-haired man wearing sunglasses, sitting on a terrace overlooking a tropical setting. He began to read aloud.

' "SAINT: Mr President, your own citizens call you a ruthless dictator. PRESIDENT: Nonsense! Whoever repeats such slander will be shot! ... Er ... I mean ... SAINT: Thank you, Mr President." '

Chamberlain chuckled. 'Well, I guess not *everybody*.'

'I don't want everybody,' Jennifer said softly, as if to herself.

Chamberlain was touched. She seemed almost passable and he stared at her with empathy. Jennifer set down her last piece of luggage. She stood in the doorway and looked into his eyes. He waited for her to speak, believing he had somehow got through.

'Look, mister,' she said. 'You helped me on board. You didn't behave like an animal. Thank you. Now, fuck off!'

Jennifer slammed the door shut, leaving Chamberlain cold in the corridor. Stunned, he looked up and down. A man was nearby doing breathing exercises by an open window. He had seen and heard everything and he looked at Chamberlain with sympathetic eyes. They exchanged wide, friendly grins.

Chamberlain returned to his compartment. The man, an over-the-hill tennis instructor named Parsons, went back to his.

Jim Parsons was travelling with Ginger Blandings, a rich but fallen actress of the 1940s, a decade older than Parsons himself.

Ginger, though frayed around the edges, was undeniably still attractive – a tide of emotions high and low but always 'on camera'. At the moment she busied herself with unpacking, while Parsons went through endless rounds of gymnastics.

'This is the kind of travel I love, darling,' she said somewhat grandiosely. 'Reminds me of Hitchcock ... of Marlene in *Shanghai Express* ... What was the line? ... "It took more than one man to change my name to Shanghai Lily".'

Parsons was unimpressed. He had heard this a million times and he had many more deep knee-bends to do.

'Well, I never was right for the part,' said Ginger.

It was time for Parsons to say something; he knew it was time.

'What kind of travel did you say you liked, Ginger?'

Ginger gestured sweepingly. 'Tête-à-tête .. Candlelight

... and whispers ...' She looked suggestively at the bed. 'The kind that lasts all night...' Parsons grimaced privately, but Ginger went on, '... and leaves scratches on my back.'

Parsons couldn't resist. 'No wonder your back's so scarred.'

Ginger tumbled into an instant depression and broke out a bottle of Seagram's from a suitcaseful. Parsons knew he had gone too far and when she had trouble opening the bottle, he helped her, despite his concern, as if that could patch things up.

'Hey, Ginger, your back's just fine,' he said tenderly. 'Real ... smooth.'

Ginger squeezed his hand gratefully but she continued to sulk.

'I was thinking of Oscar.'

'He'll be all right. Oscar's a champion.'

Ginger was suddenly indignant. 'Imagine treating a champion that way!'

*

In the baggage car, an exceedingly unhappy-looking toy poodle sat in a wicker travelling cage, a jewelled collar around his neck bearing his name: Oscar.

In another part of the car, crouched behind an assortment of crates, was Yassan ... ill, feverish.

3 12.50pm

The International Health Emergency Alert and Rescue Commission was, until its dissolution not very long ago, a top secret committee of the Security Council of the United Nations, operating under the code name, 'Milestone'. It was a twelve-member body composed of nine men and three women.

The underground meeting room of the Milestone Command Centre – it, too, recently dismantled – was spacious and highly functional. It hummed with a bank of modern electronic equipment. A team of communications personnel sat behind a glass panel. On one of the walls there was a large screen, on which, at the moment, various maps, grid lines, numbers and coloured lights were being flashed confusedly, until finally fixing on a huge map of Switzerland with a pulsating red light situated north of the town of Lausanne. Some of the Commission members looked at one another questioningly.

The doors opened. Mackenzie entered with a small entourage. There was a momentary stir, but the room soon fell deathly silent.

Mackenzie took his place. Behind him a large tape recorder was mounted on the wall. A warning sign read: 'Top Secret: Milestone Reference Only'. The machine had one switch prominently marked: 'Destruct'. A red light went on. The tape turned.

An anonymous voice can be heard on that first turn of the tape. It is hardly more than a nervous whisper: 'There are twelve hundred people on board that train, sir.'

The reply is unmistakably Mackenzie's: incisive, unhesitant, sorrowful.

'Poor unlucky people.'

Mackenzie walked to the wall screen, stopping at the pulsating light indicating the train's position. He spoke dryly, informing the members of the Commission of a situation about which they had no prior knowledge.

'We've got a suspected 3XP primary vector aboard a transcontinental train. The suspect is an unidentified male, about twenty-six, who was seen in the company of a positively diagnosed 3XP ... now deceased. The suspect is unaware of his exposure.'

Dr Gregorovius Hoffmann, a West German microbiologist who affected a red rose in his lapel and had a nervous habit of punctuating his cautious speech with the words 'of, course', spoke up with uncharacteristic urgency.

'We must stop the train and quarantine everybody on board!'

'Impossible,' Mackenzie replied. 'For the moment.'

He addressed the group gravely.

'There is no medical facility in the world prepared to properly isolate twelve hundred persons on short notice.... Worse, no country would willingly accept them. We need time for delicate negotiations. And for this we need top secrecy, as long as possible.'

This had a powerful effect on everyone, most of whom were not themselves scientists, but political representatives of their countries.

Mackenzie continued.

'Communications with the railway authorities and the Union Internationale des Chemins de Fer in Paris have been established under a Phase One cover story...'

Elena Lindstrom, scanning her copy of an instruction document distributed to the Commission now for the first time, flipped quickly to the section entitled, 'Cover Stories'. Under the heading, 'Phase One', there was a long list, each entry beginning as follows: 'Pretext One ... Pretext Two...' etc.

Mackenzie's voice echoed in her ears. 'We must try to identify the suspect, yet no one can board the train without an elaborate protective suit. That would attract attention and could create panic.'

Elena articulated what was on everyone's mind.

'But there must be a way!'

'There is,' said Mackenzie, 'if there's time.' He turned to the map. 'Secondly, we must protect the areas where the train passes.' He indicated the flashing red light. 'We've hooked onto a telestar remote sensing device. It reads the train's precise position at all times. Right now, it's nearing its first stop: Basel.... When it arrives, in about an hour, a lot of people will want to get off.... No one is getting off.'

Elena spoke again, this time with some hesitation.

'Can we make one thing clear? Are you talking about the survival of everyone on that train?'

'Dr Lindstrom,' Mackenzie said, 'I'm afraid I'm talking about the survival of all of us.'

4 1.30 pm

A party was in full swing in a second-class compartment occupied by a group of American college students returning from Israel. They had got out their guitars and various makeshift instruments, and were rapidly consuming their stock of cheap wine. Their gaiety had attracted the attention of other passengers, particularly some soldiers, who were eyeing the girls with the kind of jaw-hanging longing only barracks-dwellers know. One of them nudged his friend with a 'look-what-I-see' gesture.

What they saw was Susan Fishbein, a twenty-year-old junior from Hempstead, Long Island, who was loosening her blouse because of the heat. She was voluptuously bra-less, and there could be no mistake about it. Susan had had a terrible time on a kibbutz, and when she had complained about it to her friend Betty, seated beside her, Betty, who liked to read Hermann Hesse and collected picture post-cards, had shrugged it off, saying, 'Oh, you just didn't have any pioneer in you,' to which Susan had remarked, 'That's the trouble. I think one of them knocked me up.'

'I never saw such a crowded train,' Susan was saying now.

'Population explosion, Susan,' Betty explained. 'By the year two thousand there'll be people coming out of your pockets. It's like a time bomb.'

Susan took note of the soldier staring. She was not displeased.

'Yeah,' she said, 'but the trouble is it feels so good when you light the fuse.'

She glanced at the soldier and uncorked that effervescent smile which so provoked those pitiless, savage sperm machines she ruled in the queendom of her fantasies.

*

Yassan, in the baggage car, had opened Oscar's travelling cage and was holding the dog in his arms, stroking it tenderly. Oscar was pleased, but he suddenly began to bark, and Yassan quickly returned him to his cage and crawled to a hiding place.

Ginger Blandings, who had given Steward Tickler five traveller's cheques amounting to one hundred dollars to leave the baggage car door unlocked, in violation of international regulations, so that she might have 'visiting privileges', entered and rushed to Oscar, who was more than delighted to see her.

Ginger had put on a massive fur coat and she tucked the dog between the lining and her bosom and stole him out for a 'walk'.

*

In a first-class compartment near the centre of the train a man in the habit of a Roman Catholic priest sat at a window seat, reading the Scriptures. He seemed terribly annoyed by his collar and he continually moved his neck away from the source of irritation.

On the opposite side of the compartment, a seven-year-old English girl named Catherine Groom sat beside her middle-aged nanny, Mrs Emily Chadwick. Catherine, blowing pesky soap bubbles through a wire ring, stared openly at the priest, watching him suffer his collar. Suddenly, she whispered to her nanny but loud enough for everyone to hear.

'Mrs Chadwick, why is his neck all red?'

'His collar,' Mrs Chadwick replied in a much lower and patently embarrassed whisper. 'Now you mustn't—'

'Well, he should be used to it by now!' Catherine blurted.

The priest, whose name would never be learned, was taken with a flush of self-consciousness as everyone in the six-seat compartment turned for a look at his neck.

'I'm sorry, Father,' Mrs Chadwick apologized. 'She didn't mean to be rude.'

The priest nodded taciturnly and returned to his reading. Catherine stared at him.

*

With Oscar's head bobbing boisterously from beneath a mantle of furs, Ginger passed through the corridor of a second-class car. A Dutchwoman, returning to Amsterdam with a newborn baby her husband had never seen, stood by a window with the infant in her arms, and when the baby caught sight of Oscar, he reached out playfully. Ginger stopped and smiled at the young mother, while Oscar licked the baby's hand like a cube of sugar.

A conductor entered the corridor and Ginger went into quick retreat, returning in the direction from which she had come.

The conductor was no more the wiser. He, too, stopped to smile at the baby, who had put his hand in his mouth and was sucking hungrily.

*

Yassan was suffering a devastating hunger. He had found one of Oscar's boxes of dog biscuits and was shaking it violently. Hardly a crumb emerged, however, and he threw the empty box to the floor and left the baggage car.

His gait increasingly unsure, his tongue swelling in his mouth like the bloat of death, he headed for the dining car.

Little Catherine, waiting in the corridor for Mrs Chadwick to accompany her to the same place, was hoping for an adult's-eye view of the passing countryside from the window. She saw Yassan and asked him if he would lift her. He picked her up with some difficulty and held her in his arms. The top section of the window was open, and Catherine's blonde tresses whipped in the wind. She smiled warmly at Yassan, who broke into a fit of coughing. He put her down just as Mrs Chadwick appeared. She looked at him oddly, took Catherine firmly by the hand and hurried off.

*

Susan and the soldier she fancied had been wandering about the train looking in vain for a place where they might be alone, when they found the baggage car door unlocked. They stole inside.

They were about to fall into one another's arms, but a strange set of sounds suddenly filled them with fear. They looked around. Oscar was off in a corner devouring a plateful of food. They laughed. Then they kissed.

*

The dining car was crowded with all three classes of passengers, democracy being fortified by the custom of people being seated together regardless of whether they knew one another. The clatter of dishes and the movement of waiters trying to complete their work before the upcoming stop in Basel created an aura of not unpleasant busy-ness, and appetites seemed keen.

Ginger was lunching with Parsons, who did isometrics while waiting for his second course.

'I saw Oscar,' said Ginger.

'I thought you said the baggage cars were always locked.'

'Where Ginger Blandings goes, darling, doors open.'

'Must have cost a fancy tip.'

Ginger smiled dreamily. 'All he wanted was my autograph.'

Parsons frowned. Ginger glared at him.

*

Yassan was in the galley, which was momentarily empty. Food lay exposed everywhere. He dipped his bare hand into a pot of steaming rice, but when he was about to fill his mouth, he heard someone approaching and he bolted outside – almost colliding with Chamberlain, who was entering the dining car. Chamberlain stared directly into Yassan's curdled face, then went on his way.

A waiter came out of the kitchen, having filled a tureen with the freshly cooked rice, and slipped by Chamberlain. He carried it to a table where the priest was being given a place beside Mrs Chadwick and Catherine.

'Oh, Father,' Mrs Chadwick exclaimed, feeling honoured, if not blessed, 'do join us!'

The priest sat, seeming rather ill-at-ease. The waiter served the rice.

'I so hope you'll forgive Catherine's rudeness,' Mrs Chadwick prattled. 'She's quite excellent in her Sunday School studies.'

Catherine grimaced.

The priest was suddenly magnanimous. 'No such thing as a bad child, you know.' He quoted: ' "The fathers have eaten a sour grape, and the children's teeth are set on edge." . . . So spoke the Prophet Isaiah.'

He seemed fully pleased with himself and Mrs Chadwick was enthralled. But Catherine's eyes brightened mischievously.

'Jeremiah,' she said.

Both Mrs Chadwick and the priest were scandalized. Catherine, however, struck again.

'Chapter thirty-one, verse twenty-nine.'

The priest looked at her with half-concealed hatred. Mrs Chadwick was at a loss. The waiter came by.

'Would anyone care for more rice?'

*

Chamberlain had been ushered to a table already occupied by two nuns and Jennifer Saint. Jennifer, looking up from her food, gave him a 'not-you-again' glance, but Chamberlain bowed politely.

She returned to her meal. He sat beside her and picked up the menu.

'What's good?' he asked.

'Faith and charity,' she said, looking at the nuns, who nodded their approval.

'Are you always so pleasant?'

'A little less once a month.'

The nuns disapproved.

'You should take iron.'

'I hate pills.'

'Not pills. Nails.'

Jennifer tried hard, but even she could not help but laugh, and when she did the nuns smiled broadly at Chamberlain's victory. He grinned, too. Their eyes met and a moment of warmth was exchanged between them.

*

Jonathan Chamberlain had suddenly become important at the Milestone Command Centre. Steward Tickler, receiving an unexplained query, via the radio-telephone communications setup in the postal car, as to whether there were any doctors on board the train, had passed on Chamberlain's name, and now Elena Lindstrom was riffling through the pages of the publication, *Who's Who in Medicine*.

She stood at the bank of computers with Mackenzie, both of them beside a seated programmer, who awaited their instructions at a card coding machine. Beside them was a tray of sandwiches and soft drinks. Elena and the programmer were eating, but Mackenzie hadn't touched his food.

'Here it is,' said Elena, finding the entry. 'Chamberlain, Jonathan ... surgeon ... born 1932 ... son of Philip and ...'

'Unimportant,' said the programmer as he launched into the coding process. 'Just his medical school, residency training, and present hospital affiliation.'

The machine had been programmed on the basis of the Benjamin principle. It had been Marcus Benjamin, a French disciple of Durkheimian sociology, who as far back as the 1930s had postulated, if not boasted, 'Tell me a man's country, his job, and his father's job, and I'll tell you his dreams.' It was a blasphemous idea at the time, men then being thought of by science, not to mention some religions, as unfathomably complex entities, each of which was, and ever would be, unique. But Benjamin had refused to be intimidated by revered beliefs in individuality, and had gone on to prove his heretical principle. We are all individuals, he conceded, but only as no two leaves on the same tree are exactly alike. Men are the leaves on a social tree. 'Show me the species, I'll draw you the leaves.'

As challenging men usually earn more wrath than honour, Benjamin was predictably insulted, oppressed and finally ignored by a generation of poetic sociology, only to be rediscovered – long after his Reichian-like death in a Paris jail – by the amoral inclinations of unbaptized computers, which, in the case of the Milestone programme, spoke thusly: 'Show me his medical school, residency training, and present hospital affiliation, and I'll print out his soul.' What's more, with an accuracy running upwards of 99.9 per cent, it worked.

Elena scanned. 'Harvard ... Harvard ... and ... uh ... Harvard.' She turned to Mackenzie. 'Looks like we're in luck.'

Mackenzie was sceptical. The programmer ran the card through the computer, which, capable of handling 100 million operations per second, began to print out immediately. He tore the paper from the machine and handed it to Elena, who glanced at it and reported to Mackenzie.

'He's in the ninety percentile group.' Referring to an explanatory chart, she read out some key words: 'Intelligent ... competent ... reliable ... coolheaded,' and added her own spot assessment, 'and probably charming.'

'So's my grandmother,' Mackenzie retorted, looking at the printout. 'What does this mean? "A-T correlation zero-zero-nine".'

Elena consulted the chart. '"Highly motivated by own judgements, rather than mere authority".'

'Sounds like he thinks.'

There was concern in his voice. Mackenzie regarded any possible threat to his own authority as potentially dangerous to Milestone, and Elena understood that. He stared abstractedly at the tray of food in front of him.

'Shall I call back?'

Mackenzie hesitated for a moment.

'Call back.'

He pushed his food away brusquely. He wondered about this Harvard-Harvard-Harvard, this thinking, competent data bit named Chamberlain, or 0101111111110010101100 on the binary code. There was something about the Benjamin principle, and even more so its computerized model, which Mackenzie found repulsive, in spite of, or perhaps because of, its impeccable reliability. There were atavistic quirks in Mackenzie, and often as now they felt like rosebush thorns in his gut. A man *was* the sum of an infinite number of uniquenesses, though they were relevant only to the man and the poets. There was a real human being on that train out there who had been present on this planet for more than forty years, and now there was a newborn behavioural pulse riding the computer circuit mocking his individuality, running around and saying things like, 'Show me his shirt size and I'll hand you his balls,' and getting away with it by the simple, outrageous reason of being right. What was so great about being right? Mackenzie thought.

He picked up the *Who's Who*, which still lay open at Chamberlain's page. '...son of Philip and Elizabeth Harrison'. Who were these people? And what were they doing in New Mexico having children, anyway? '...married, Aug 1956, Deborah Putnam (BA Vassar, Jun 1956).' Now *there* was a clue: a New England 1950s-model WASP, no doubt, getting her lilywhite mitts on a promising boy from the mountains (note how they waited for her to get her degree before marrying). How did they fare? he mused. 'Children: Philip (Dec 1956)...' Aha! '...James (Sept 1960); divorced, Oct 1965...' Enough! he thought. The book knew far less than the computer. In the end, a rational man would have to turn with praise to Marcus Benjamin, unless a rational man were the subject of his principle.

*

With hardly more than a kernel of rice for all his efforts, Yassan returned to the baggage car only to have his eyes gorged with the plate Ginger had set for Oscar. By now, however, it had been licked clean, but Oscar was busy in his cage with a meaty calf's bone.

Yassan stared at the food. Oscar quickly became aware and began to growl menacingly. Salivating, Yassan tried to reach into the cage and snatch the bone from the dog. Oscar snapped at his hand. The bone fell out of the open cage. Yassan lunged for it. Oscar sunk his teeth into his arm. Yassan recoiled in a wail of pain, but the dog shielded his possession, leering venomously.

Yassan dropped to his knees wearily, with the realization that he had been vanquished by the dog. He stared at him enviously. Oscar chewed.

5 2.17pm

The train suddenly came to a jolting stop.

In the dining car, trays of food flew forward. Passengers were thrown from their seats and were splattered with whatever they had been eating. There were angry cries in a babel of languages, but they quickly subsided when a few passengers looked out the windows, drawing the attention of everyone, including Chamberlain and Jennifer Saint.

Jennifer did not need more than a glimpse before she turned and left to gather up her gear.

Outside, on a scrubby stretch of countryside, the train was slowly being surrounded by a heavily armed contingent of state police. Several jeeps patrolled alongside the train, as well as two or three ambulances, their rotary lights flashing red and amber. None of the vehicles, however, came within a fifty-foot belt of no-man's-land formed by the cordon of police.

The passengers stared out in bewildered silence. They were unaware that a railroad car was being moved down the tracks towards the end of the train. The new car, pushed by an electric locomotive in reverse, was coupled to the rear of the train. The locomotive moved off. Inside the new car was an armed escort of eighteen security police, who would accompany the train until Milestone moved again.

*

Jennifer moved through the corridors photographing the police manoeuvres outside and the passengers watching them. Most people, she saw, were simply confused and puzzled, and there was very little hint of fear. Indeed, some were amused by the whole affair, as when she happened to pass two of the American college youths. Betty was joking with Tom, a black student from Philadelphia.

'We've been hijacked, man,' she said, smiling.

'Fantastic! I've never been to Cuba.'

Jennifer moved on. Kaplan was being chided by a fellow passenger named Gunther.

'Hey, Kaplan, maybe they heard your ticking suitcase!'

Everyone laughed. Kaplan, however, had his riposte at the ready.

'I'll tell you thing, *amigo*. Time flies ... but a good watch goes by train.'

Up came a handful of watches for sale.

As Jennifer went about the train, many passengers grew bored with the events outside and returned to their seats, while others paid no attention at all to the matter at hand. They smoked, ate, read, slept, and a few lovers were necking. Others, realizing they were being photographed, broke into the standard poses: silly grins, stony faces, and not a little ham.

'It's the fuel shortage,' some were saying. Others attributed the unscheduled stop to 'drugs'.

A tiny man with a fat wife stormed past Jennifer, the woman scolding her husband.

'Why did I ever let you take me to this Europe?'

The man shrugged at Jennifer, who smiled ingratiatingly.

Jennifer felt strangely exhilarated, sensing that the Nikon was working well gave her energy. Suddenly, however, her viewfinder framed Yassan among the crowd and he stared transfixedly into the camera.

His eyes were watery and shot with blood. He seemed hypnotized or charmed, frozen. But he quickly turned away and Jennifer looked at him oddly as he disappeared.

Jennifer came to the end of the train. There were hardly any other passengers there. She leaned out the window and saw the newly attached security car and some of the armed escort. Perplexed, she worked nonetheless. One of the police, a young recruit, it seemed, had come down from the security car and was smoking a cigarette.

Jennifer leaned very far from the open window and began to photograph him. He motioned to her to get back in, and when she paid him no mind, he lifted his sub-machine gun and pointed it at her menacingly. She photographed it all.

Suddenly he swung the weapon violently, smashing her camera and sending it flying from her hands. Jennifer grabbed the muzzle of his gun. She was incensed.

'Sonofabitch!'

Still holding the weapon, she stared down the barrel defiantly. Another guard approached them, his gun drawn. Jennifer pushed the muzzle away in a gesture of disgust and walked off.

*

Chamberlain was still in the dining car when Jennifer passed through and he immediately took note of her unusually subdued appearance.

A moment later, the train began to move. The passengers broke into a rousing cheer and applause, rupturing the accumulated tension. Everyone was all smiles. Chamberlain, too, was relieved. There was a general return to normal, passengers going back to their tables, waiters bringing out rich desserts, which would be served 'on the house'.

The nuns, however, did not come back and Chamberlain was left alone with Jennifer, who now seemed the only one in low spirits.

'You look like my patients before they go under the knife,' Chamberlain said, peering into her eyes.

Jennifer turned to him, though she was still lost in thought.

'We're all under a knife,' she replied enigmatically.

Chamberlain looked at her oddly. He was about to say something else when he was interrupted by Steward Tickler, who whispered to him:

'Dr Chamberlain, could you come with me, sir ... An emergency.'

Chamberlain saw concern in his face. He nodded, and turned to Jennifer.

'Excuse me.'

He left. Jennifer began to fit the pieces together.

Outside, the country was swiftly giving way to the city. The train began to slow. Traffic thickened. Shrubbery turned to walls of stone. A road sign stood wide and tall: Basel.

6 2.44pm

Mackenzie and Elena were in the telecommunications area behind a plate glass panel. Mackenzie was in mid-conversation with Chamberlain via the radio-telephone link with the train.

'Not "if", doctor, *when*! He's on that train, gasping, coughing, and shivering with a fever over a hundred and five ... But let me speak frankly, Chamberlain. Seven minutes ago we had a computer projection that if the suspect is not off that train in one hundred and eighty-two minutes, there is zero gain by his removal. The total pathogenic biomass will have accumulated to the point where any further delay would have net negative effects.' He breathed deeply. 'You identify him, we'll get him off.'

Chamberlain, in the train's postal operations unit, replied, looking at his watch.

'In other words, you have two hours and fifty-five minutes.'

'*You* have two hours and fifty-five minutes. Or he stays! ... Chamberlain, there are thirteen passenger cars, two hundred and four compartments. That leaves you less than ten seconds for each person. You have a lot of patients to see, doctor.'

This irritated Chamberlain. 'What care are you prepared to provide the others?' He listened for a moment then replied angrily, 'All right, provide *us*.'

'What would *you* do, Chamberlain?' Mackenzie asked. It was a test and he was not unimpressed with the man's response. 'Yes, yes,' said Mackenzie. 'We are working on it. I await your call...' He pressed an electronic calculator and read the figures. 'Before five-forty-one this afternoon.'

He hung up. Elena studied him.

'Well, is he "competent, reliable, intelligent", etcetera?'

'He thinks,' said Mackenzie worriedly.

*

Kaplan was speaking philosophically to Gunther, who was busy getting his bags together.

'One thing you should know about Basel, *amigo*: chemicals. Antibiotics, plastics, synthetics. I knew a guy who made a fortune in hair dye ... Getting off here?'

Gunther nodded and stepped into the corridor.

'*Guten Reise, amigo*,' he said with a note of sarcasm. He was not a pleasant man, and Kaplan, though he spoke German fluently, looked uneasy hearing someone else use the language. He shuddered, relieved that Gunther was going.

The corridor outside was full of passengers intending to detrain at Basel. A conductor entered the car and called out the station. He was followed by Chamberlain, who forced his way through the crowd, studying faces in search of the suspect. One thing he knew for certain: the train was not going to stop. Indeed, it picked up speed now, and it did not take very long for the passengers to realize that they were bypassing the city.

Angry voices soon began to swell – remarks such as:

'But I've got to get off!'

'This could never happen in England!'

'I shall report this to the tourist bureau!'

'I'll lose my hotel reservations!'

Tom, Betty and Susan, all of whom had been planning to get off, moved further down the corridor, where a conductor was trying to calm irate passengers. One old woman was sobbing. She was dressed in her Sunday clothes, wore a straw hat, a veil, and her cheeks were heavily rouged.

'Nothing to worry about,' the conductor 'explained'. 'Technical difficulties. You'll be given free lodging in Paris, and return transportation.'

'I can't go to Paris, man!' Tom said, winking to his friends. 'I don't have enough clean underwear!'

This brought a laugh from the other students, but the mood changed quickly as the old woman began to wail.

'I have to go to a funeral ... My son ...'

She cried uncontrollably. Susan tried to comfort her.

*

In the first-class compartment occupied by the priest, sounds of protest coming from the corridor were clearly disturbing him. Mrs Chadwick, however, babbled to him endlessly.

'You'll adore Brussels, Father. It's so, so ... Belgian!'

The priest nodded distractedly, glancing at his watch and wiping his brow with a huge, coloured handkerchief.

The compartment door slid open. Chamberlain entered with Steward Tickler.

'The train is bypassing Basel,' said the steward, while Chamberlain surveyed the passengers. 'Nothing serious.'

The priest suddenly leaped to his feet and hurried past them, leaving the compartment. Mrs Chadwick seemed bewildered.

'He said he was going to Brussels.'

Chamberlain looked around. Catherine, too, had something to say about the priest.

'I don't like him.'

Chamberlain backed out, as Mrs Chadwick reprimanded the little girl.

*

Tom, Betty and Susan were tossing their gear back into their compartment.

'So we go to Paris,' Susan said uncaringly. 'I always wanted to see the Leaning Tower.'

Tom looked at her in utter disbelief, but Susan had her eye on a sailor no more than ten feet away. They exchanged smiles. Betty was reproachful.

'I don't know, Betty,' Susan remarked, 'every time I see a man in uniform, I get a funny feeling between my toes.'

Betty was curious. 'Which toes?'

'The big ones!' Tom answered for her, his indiscreet but friendly grin revealing how well he really knew her.

Susan looked at him trying to fathom what he had meant, but the microspan of her concentration powers ran out, and, giving up, she flashed another of those semen-boiler smiles at the sailor, who began to move closer.

The tiny man and his fat wife were charging through the corridor. Apparently they too had wanted to get off in Basel, since the wife was fuming. This time, however, the man, doing his best to keep pace with her, spoke up timidly.

'Why did you ever let me take you to this Europe?'

'Shut up!' said the wife.

The man shrugged helplessly, tagging after her.

*

In the diaphragm connecting bridge between two cars, Jennifer caught up with Chamberlain. They had to shout to hear one another because of the high level of noise on the bridge.

'I was looking for you!' she cried at the top of her lungs.

'You found me!'

'What's the big emergency?'

'I have to make some house calls!'

He left hurriedly. She followed him into the car, stopping him by the arm.

'Listen, Chamberlain! I've been through three wars, nine

revolutions, and a hundred mine fields! It's my job and today's a weekday ... I'm coming along. Friend or enemy!'

Chamberlain studied her intensely. He was drawn to her, wanting to trust her.

'Friend?' he asked finally.

Jennifer hesitated. She looked deep into his eyes, then spoke decisively.

'Friend.'

Chamberlain said nothing. He turned. She followed. Chamberlain looked at his watch. He shook his head forlornly. He briefed her quickly as he would a colleague on entering an operating chamber. She was sober, her professional self, though her innards coiled – the sclerosis of combat she had come to know. She immediately told him about the security car that had been coupled to the train, and of her experience with the guard.

'Was there anyone else around?' Chamberlain asked. 'Someone who might have become frightened and have had reason to hide?'

Jennifer shook no, but then her eyes slowly brightened with recollection.

'There was this face,' she said. 'In my camera ... helpless ... shaking ... coughing ... friendless.'

As she spoke, Chamberlain himself seemed to be recalling. An adulterated face. The young man in the galley. Chamberlain straightened in a posture of command.

'You start at the top again!' he cried. 'I'll work towards you from the other end! Look in every corner! In every damn toilet!'

7 4.50pm

Mackenzie was speaking with some of the Commission members at the wall screen showing the train's position: it had crossed the Rhine and had entered French territory.

Dr Hoffmann, glancing through his instruction document, seemed disturbed.

'If I read this right, Mackenzie,' he said angrily, 'you have the power to act for the one hundred and thirty-six governments of the United Nations any way you see fit ... including, for all we know, blowing up that train.'

'Correct ... In the name of collective security.'

Everyone was horrified, including Elena.

'That puts us strictly in an advisory role,' Hoffmann continued. 'Why should we help you play God?'

'I'm not "playing" anything,' Mackenzie flared. 'I'm acting under a legal mandate from the Security Council!'

He seemed shaken. Hoffmann was not satisfied.

'Then what do you want from *us*?'

Mackenzie took hold of himself. 'I'm under no obligation to take your advice. But that doesn't mean I won't need it.' He turned to the group. His voice was sincere. 'I assure you, after five forty-one this evening ... I'll need it.'

*

At exactly 4.57 a helicopter bearing the insignia of the Red Cross lifted into the afternoon sky.

*

Kaplan had once again set up shop in the corridor and had drawn a sizeable crowd around him.

'Here, *messieurs*, *mesdames*,' he cried, holding up his wares, 'Superwatch! ... Used by spacemen, frogmen and common men.... Now you see it ... Now you *see* it!' The same magician's flourish as before, but this time it did not disappear. "*Meine Herren, meine Damen. Je vous voudrais dire...*'

49

Kaplan went on and on. Chamberlain, perspiration rising across the surface of his skin, pushed by him, rapidly exhausting every possibility. Less than a half-hour remained, and it was no longer possible for him to believe that even with Jennifer's help eye-to-eye contact could be made with every face on that train. The sheer geography of the three-foot corridor widths, cluttered to one extent or another by restless passengers, slowed his efforts to little more than a frustrating crawl. Yet, they had narrowed the field to one face in particular. But where?

He had seen him come out of the galley, Chamberlain thought, taxing his deductive faculties; which meant he probably had no money to buy food. Most likely he was in second class, and perhaps, it occurred to him as he poked his head into one compartment after another, he had not even been able to buy a ticket and was wandering from one hiding place to another. But how? The toilets; he was checking them scrupulously. The dining car? He had searched it. Communications? Impossible. The baggage car? It was surely locked. Yet . . . He headed for the baggage car.

*

In one of the two wagon-lits cars, Jennifer, continuing her half of the search, came to a compartment where a young man in a tuxedo, with a loosened collar, stood at the partly open door. Jennifer saw a woman's crossed legs inside, a bridal veil lying beside her on the bed. The groom looked nervous.

'How far you going?' Jennifer asked, trying to cover her interest in peering inside. The groom winked at her with false bravura.

'All the way, ma'am. . . . All the way.'

An impatient voice called out from the compartment.

'Alfred . . .'

The groom seemed a little less confident now. Jennifer shored up his courage.

'Make haste,' she said with a fleeting smile, '...slowly.'

Jennifer left him as he closed himself inside, her expression fading to deep concern as she became aware of passing time.

*

The pilot of the Red Cross helicopter, an obsolete Westland Whirlwind, blade-flapped for more surface area and brought his air speed over the 200 mph line. He looked down. The Transcontinental Express was crossing the vineyards of Champagne, a glittering necklace on green velvet. He was gaining on it fast and now he pitched his blades to sharpen his angle of attack.

*

The baggage room was clearly marked that international regulations prohibited any access while the train was in motion. Chamberlain tried the door. It was locked. He put his ear to the wall. It seemed to him he heard movement inside, but he could not be sure that it was no more than the steady rocking of the train. Was it worth finding a conductor and having the room opened, killing how many precious minutes? He had not yet decided when he spotted a slight-looking man walking unsteadily, stumbling away from him in the next corridor. He seemed to be holding his stomach. Chamberlain took after him, seized him, and spun him around. He was an older man, who appeared ready to take strenuous offence, but he suddenly put his hand to his mouth, gagged, and dashed to the toilet. Chamberlain recognized the unmistakable pallor, cold sweating and nausea of simple motion sickness.

He looked at his watch. His jaw clenched. In twelve minutes time would be up. He gave up the conductor idea and moved towards the rear of the train where the odds, however long, were in theory rather better. There were still two or three cars to be double-checked – too many to waste time on the baggage car gamble.

*

In the baggage room, Susan, who had bolted the door from the inside, was having a go with the navy. She and the sailor stood entwined in a corner of her favourite trysting place. It was hardly a re-enactment of her fantasies, but it was better than Hermann Hesse.

They turned, or rather, wriggled, in search of a more pleasurable position. Susan opened her eyes momentarily. She had wanted to see if his were closed. Unlike the wicked machines they were, but she was met with a terrifying sight and she froze.

Standing only a few inches away, partially hidden by a crate, was Yassan. He leaned against the wall like a plank of yellow wood. His chest heaved. His mouth was brittle, his swollen tongue protruding.

Though the sailor was still unaware of what had happened, Susan was about to scream. Yassan's hand went up and clamped over her mouth, as he looked at her with pathetic eyes.

The sailor wheeled around. Susan, thinking herself in bodily danger, bit hard on Yassan's hand. He drew back. The sailor was ready for knightly attack, but Yassan collapsed.

Susan and the sailor stared dumbfoundedly at the fallen man. She saw his hand. Her teeth marks were visible and it trickled blood.

*

Mackenzie stood at the wall screen showing the train's position. He threw a nervous glance at the clock. It read 5.33. Eight minutes remained. He looked at Elena. She seemed under a strain. He drew a breath.

*

Yassan lay unconscious on the floor. Oscar had got out of his cage and stood beside him. The dog nudged, as if trying to wake him. Oscar whimpered. He needed help.

*

Ginger sat at a mirror, combing out her hair.

'Should I visit Oscar?' she asked, sipping rye. 'It's five thirty-five. Over an hour. Lord knows, he may need me desperately.'

Parsons lay on the bed reading the European edition of *Time* magazine. He did toe exercises.

'Says here Europeans travelling by rail covered over twenty billion miles last year.' He contemplated for a moment. 'And where did it all get them?'

'Frankly, my dear,' said Ginger, 'I don't give a damn.'

Parsons shot up. 'That was Gable in *Gone with the Wind* ... right?'

Ginger nodded. 'But I'll bet you don't know what Lord Olivier said to me when I told him I was doing Blanche DuBois in *Streetcar*?'

Parsons was stumped. 'What did he say?'

Ginger did an Oxonian basso worthy of the Old Vic.

'Frankly, my dear, I don't give a damn.'

They laughed. But Ginger fell sullen. She began to drink again.

'Why don't you go visit Oscar?' Parsons suggested.

*

Chamberlain despaired. He was dripping sweat, tiring, and he felt his in-one-out-the-other hunt a sterile drudge. His intrusions were being met with discomfiting annoyance, even indignation, and the panoply of irate faces was fusing into an ugly neuter composite. He wondered if he would still recognize the man he had seen, and it was possible, he thought, that he was the wrong man in any case; that the suspect in question had gone unnoticed before his burning eyes. There were under five minutes left and he knew that in even less time he would catch up with Jennifer and there would be no place more to turn ... unless she had better luck than he.

Jennifer, in the next car coming nearer, had had none.

*

Holding up two watches and setting them at 5.37, Kaplan was coming to the end of his spiel.

'My friends, at long last, Superwatch! ... All-American design, made in Deutschland and Japan. The glory, if not the meaning of our times!'

He stepped into the thoroughly delighted crowd, offering the watches, but the passengers began to drift away, rapidly losing interest.

As a last resort, he opened his coat wide, displaying all sorts of items for sale, hanging in neat little rows from the lining of his jacket. His arms extended in a Christ-like spread. There were charms, rosary beads and razor blades. No one cared.

*

Chamberlain's and Jennifer's paths had converged at the compartment of the college youths. They had seen instantly in one another's eyes that both had failed. Now, inside, Chamberlain queried the students hard.

'He was in his mid-twenties, in a state of semi-collapse.'

The students looked at one another. Susan sat quietly in a corner staring straight ahead.

'He's fuzz,' said Tom.

Chamberlain exploded. He grabbed Tom by his shirt and drove him up against the window, almost dislodging Susan from her seat. His fist was buried in Tom's throat.

'I'm a physician and people's lives are in danger!' he cried, tightening his grip on Tom's windpipe. 'Including yours!'

'Okay, man,' Tom gasped.

Chamberlain released his hold. Tom spoke soberly.

'I just didn't want to see anyone ripped off, that's all.' He turned to the others. 'We didn't see any sickies, did we?'

There was a general negative reaction.

'Sorry, doc,' Tom said earnestly.

Chamberlain nodded in resignation and started to leave, but Jennifer had her eyes on Susan.

'See anyone?'

Susan was terrorstricken. She hesitated, choked.

'I ... I ...'

*

Mackenzie and everyone else stared at the overhead clock. There were about two minutes left. Mackenzie traded looks with the radio operator, who shook his head no.

*

Chamberlain, Jennifer and the steward hurried towards the baggage car door. Ginger was coming out of the room, looking troubled. She saw the three of them rushing towards her and appeared frightened. Jennifer turned to Chamberlain.

'These doors should be locked!'

Ginger looked at the steward. Guilt rose in his eyes, but suddenly a groan of human pain emerged from inside the room.

'Wait outside!' Chamberlain cried.

He entered the baggage compartment and saw Yassan. He had regained consciousness but he still lay on the floor, and he looked up at Chamberlain with eyes that pleaded for help. Chamberlain took note of his coated tongue. He palpated under Yassan's armpits and in the area around his groin. He leaped to his feet.

'Steward!' he shouted hoarsely.

He ran to the door, Yassan's pitiful stare following his every move. The steward appeared, but he shrank back at the sight of Yassan.

'Call Mackenzie!' cried Chamberlain.

The steward looked at his watch. 'But there's less than a minute left, sir.'

'Call him!'

Chamberlain looked back at Yassan, and for the first time

he saw the dog. His eyes were pinned to the animal, for Oscar, too, appeared sick. Chamberlain approached. The dog was passive, trembling.

*

At Milestone, the final seconds were being devoured by the clock. Mackenzie looked to the communications panel. The radio operator shook no. The clock struck 5.41. Mackenzie picked up the intercom microphone to the panel.

'Recall the helicopter.'

The operator nodded. Mackenzie turned to the wall screen and began to approach a projected cutaway drawing of the train.

'At this stage,' he said to the group, 'the Milestone—'

He was interrupted by a voice on the intercom.

'Chamberlain is on the phone, sir,' said the operator, with a voice that betrayed his emotion. 'They've found the suspect!'

Among the Commission members a sigh of relief was raised.

Mackenzie lifted the radio-telephone.

'Too late, Chamberlain. There's nothing to gain any more.'

'There's plenty to gain!' Chamberlain pleaded from the other end, as Jennifer listened on an extension line. 'What you lose you'll make up by his removal. No computer in the world can tell what these people will do when they know what's going on! ... Better not have a scapegoat in their hands.'

Mackenzie was struck by this argument. He studied the clock, then spoke decisively.

'We'll remove the suspect.'

8 5.42 pm

The pilot of the rescue helicopter listened on his headset. He turned to the co-pilot and motioned to something behind them. The co-pilot reached for a pair of white hoods, goggles and deflection masks, like those worn in the isolation chamber. They were putting them on when the co-pilot pointed urgently to the instrument panel. A red light was flashing.

*

Elena, in touch with the radio operator, caught Mackenzie's eye.

'Rescue reports fuel problem if the operation is delayed much longer,' she said.

Mackenzie frowned.

'They're over the train,' said Elena. 'Shall I have them stop it now?'

'I'm trying to prevent panic, not encourage it,' Mackenzie said sharply. 'Our security escort can't handle a situation like this. We don't want any jumpers, or a bloody stampede! No one gets off except the suspect!'

Elena conveyed the message.

*

The door to the baggage car was wide open. The onrushing wind swirled. The sound of the helicopter could be heard overhead, and the rescue harness dangled from the sky.

'Put the dog on first!' Jennifer shouted to Chamberlain. 'These things need practice!'

'Practice?' Ginger cried horrifiedly.

Chamberlain agreed. Parsons tried to calm Ginger, who was crying her farewells to Oscar. Yassan lay motionless on the steel floor.

Ginger tried to shield the dog. He barked weakly. Jennifer held Ginger back, as Parsons joined Chamberlain in helping to attach the wicker basket to the harness.

'Don't worry, Oscar honey,' Ginger sobbed. 'Be brave! Think of ... of ... think of Rin-Tin-Tin!'

The co-pilot, wearing the complete suit of protective clothing, began to lift the harness. The red light on the instrument panel flashed on his goggles.

Oscar rose swiftly, Ginger blowing kisses after him.

'I wish I owned half that dog,' Parsons murmured. Chamberlain looked at him questioningly. 'I'd have left my half at home.'

The two men began to move Yassan towards the open door, waiting for the harness to return. Yassan stared up at them with a mixture of gratitude and unspeakable fear.

*

Mackenzie, following the rescue in the communications section, stood over the radio operator.

'How's the fuel situation?' he asked.

'Looks good. About five minutes. ... They got the dog off.'

Mackenzie was incredulous. 'The what?'

The operator shrugged. Mackenzie was pensive, interested.

*

The train's fireman came into the locomotive cab. The engineer turned to him.

'They're getting him off now,' said the fireman.

The engineer nodded, studying the road ahead. Suddenly his eyes widened.

'They better,' he said.

The fireman was puzzled. The engineer motioned to him to look straight ahead. The fireman stared out of the forward window. His jaw dropped.

'Bloody Jesus!'

*

Her hair flapping in the wind, Jennifer leaned from the train, trying to grab the rescue harness, while Chamberlain and Parsons lifted Yassan to a standing position.

The harness was slightly beyond Jennifer's reach. Cursing

under her breath, she struggled vainly in apparent danger of falling from the train. Suddenly, she thrust one hand to Chamberlain, motioning to him to hold it.

'Don't just stand there!' she shouted.

Chamberlain locked her hand in his, and leaning much further now, she seized the harness. Parsons and Chamberlain moved Yassan into the apparatus quickly. But the entire device was yanked violently from their hands and then Yassan was thrown. He fell at Jennifer's feet.

The harness scraped across the steel floor, banging against the open doorway. It took off for the sky above as if propelled by a power all its own. Gone.

Everyone was stunned. They leaned out and looked up: the helicopter was soaring, turning in retreat.

Jennifer was still searching the sky, as if for understanding, when Chamberlain turned his head in the direction the train was moving. The explanation was looming up ahead perilously: the black mouth of a tunnel bored through the heart of an enormous mountain, and the train was on a one-way-only course headed through.

'Watch out!' he cried, grabbing Jennifer and pulling her to him.

They fell backward. The train drove into the tunnel, plunging them into total darkness.

The service lights went on as the train continued through the tunnel. In the priest's compartment, everyone but he was more or less dozing. He listened in a sweat as sounds of protest began to rise again in the corridor outside. It was rapidly becoming known that the train was bypassing Paris, too.

'I've got to be in Paris!'

'What the hell is going on?'

'Be calm, be calm...'

The priest got up and reached for a small suitcase above him. As he took it down, the sleeve of his cassock fell back dropping to about his elbow. On his muscular forearm was a tattoo of a naked woman.

He saw his arm exposed. Covering it, he whipped around wondering whether anyone had noticed. Only little Catherine's eyes were on him. He stared at her. She closed her lids, pretending sleep.

Kaplan, too, heard the angry voices outside. He was half asleep.

'Paris ... Shmaris,' he muttered to himself. 'It's all the same.'

Gunther rose from his seat anxiously, tapping the crystal of his watch with his right forefinger.

'Not if you had an important appointment in Basel over an hour ago!'

Kaplan regarded the man's plight mildly, and he gestured grandiosely.

'All the world's an oyster, Shakespeare once said.' Then, reflecting a moment, he added, 'But I'll tell you one thing, *amigo*. It's better to be inside than out.'

Gunther observed him oddly.

'What's your business, anyway? Selling watches to tourists?'

'At the height of the tourist season, I sell anything that sells,' Kaplan replied, his sad, wise eyes gleaming. 'In the dead season, I pray for the dead – for a fee.'

He sank into troubled sleep.

9 6.03 pm

On the wall screen at the Milestone Command Centre, there was a projection of a fourteenth-century drawing showing a crucifix held over a group of Jews being burned for having 'poisoned the wells'.

'Can you hear me, Dr Chamberlain?' Mackenzie was saying into a microphone being adjusted by a workman.

The image on the wall screen flashed to another early woodcut of boarded-up houses and human bodies piled in a village square.

'Not very well,' Chamberlain's voice, being transmitted through the Milestone intercom system, replied.

The workman linking the transmission from the train nodded to Mackenzie to try again.

'That better?' Mackenzie asked.

'Fine,' Chamberlain was heard to say, his voice extremely clear.

Mackenzie motioned to the communications panel. A Milestone document numbered 72/438A and entitled 'Pandemic Dynamics' was flashed on the wall screen [see reproduction on following pages].

All of the Commission members were in their places, taut with anticipation. They studied the chart, which was a kind of graph correlating well-known historical events – beginning with the fall of the Roman empire in AD 476 and on through the modern world population explosion, massive urbanization, and environmental crises – with the incidence of pandemic disease. The general tendency of the graph created a display of hills and valleys reaching ever higher peaks, and the apex projected for the present to the end of this century was shown as a great unknown, although it was clear to the Commission members that Mackenzie was about to furnish a theory.

The chart, which was stamped TOP SECRET! ALL CLEARANCE THROUGH S. MACKENZIE ONLY!, could not of course be seen by Chamberlain, who waited at the radio-telephone in the communications car.

He waited, too, for Jennifer, and when she entered, she nodded to him affirmatively, mouthing the words, 'He's resting.'

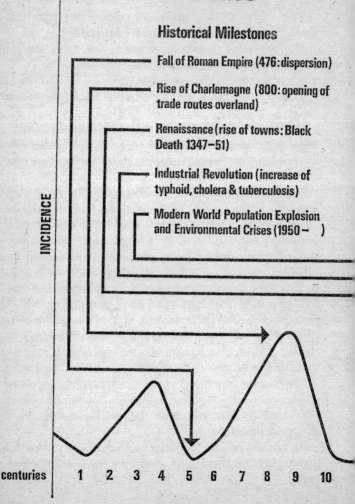

PANDEMIC DYNAMICS

Historical Milestones

Fall of Roman Empire (476 : dispersion)

Rise of Charlemagne (800 : opening of trade routes overland)

Renaissance (rise of towns : Black Death 1347–51)

Industrial Revolution (increase of typhoid, cholera & tuberculosis)

Modern World Population Explosion and Environmental Crises (1950 –   )

INCIDENCE

centuries 1 2 3 4 5 6 7 8 9 10

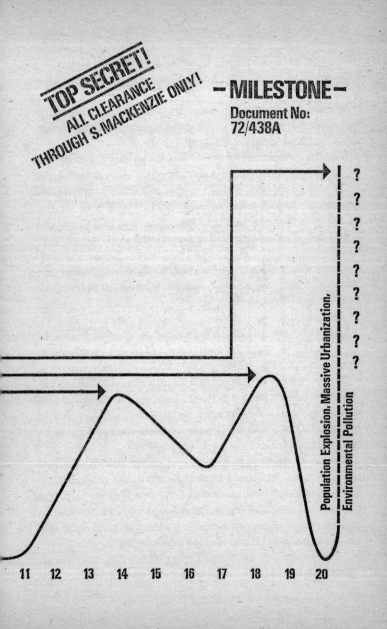

An empty wagon-lit compartment had been made available to Yassan, and when she had left him, he lay in a tortured half-delirium, but he seemed very much alive.

Now, Chamberlain handed Jennifer an auxiliary phone and she sat beside him.

Mackenzie, standing erectly, his frame struck in sharp silhouette like a minted coin by the light of the wall screen chart, began. He spoke precisely, grimly.

'The Black Death,' he said, 'wiped out one third of the world's population. Were something like it to occur again ... life on this planet, which has grown infinitely more interdependent, would suffer consequences on the scale of the Flood or a nuclear war. No less than one billion people would die.... We believe this very threat is riding on that train.'

There was a moment of silence. Only the sound of the train, filtering through the amplified radio-telephone link with Chamberlain, could be heard. It had an unsettling effect on everyone.

Mackenzie pointed to the document on the wall screen, to the heading, 'Population Explosion, Massive Urbanization, Environmental Pollution'.

'Until the work of Langer and Bernstein and others, in the late nineteen-sixties, we believed that the Black Death and similar epidemics disappeared because of so-called progress in so-called civilization.... Now we know the *opposite* to be true.'

Mackenzie glanced at Elena. She had worked with Langer and Bernstein, had never been schooled in the theories they had refuted. In a way, he envied her, for he felt that she was free of the burden of old doctrines, and was in a position to make a contribution to science he believed himself incapable of. She saw his eyes. She nodded encouragingly.

' "Progress",' he went on, hitting the word with irony, 'alters the ecology. It explains the *rise* not the fall of epidemics. Shifts in the natural environment ... new concentrations of more and more people. *Milestones*. And at every milestone, the cycle of death begins again.'

His audience, both at Milestone and on the train, hung on his words. Still, Chamberlain was sceptical.

'We have accumulating evidence,' Mackenzie continued. 'Isolated cases with increasing frequency. A new, drug-resistant germ. And now ... that train.'

Chamberlain's voice suddenly filled the room with metallic, electronic tones.

'We've been hearing all kinds of doomsday predictions for years, Mackenzie,' he said severely. 'What makes yours any better?'

Mackenzie replied with strength. 'We're here to try to stop a medical disaster, which is not, I repeat, *not* inevitable. We have alternatives.... It all depends on what we do with the Transcontinental Express.'

This brought a respectful silence. Mackenzie threw a quick nod towards the communications panel, and the cutaway scale drawing of the train appeared instantly on the wall screen. Mackenzie walked up to it.

'First,' he said determinedly, 'we seal the train.'

Chamberlain's voice interrupted again.

'If you seal the train, Mackenzie, you seal the fate of everyone on board. The conditions for contagion are already more than ideal. Even the common 'flu could become a killer.'

He spoke with a passion which had a strange effect on Jennifer, who surveyed him with intense eyes. She had seen a thousand life-and-death dramas enacted in her presence, and many times her own life, her own soul, had been on the line. But she had never felt like this. A man had entered her life and an indefinable power was winding their lives together like a helix.

'Unless we're removed to adequate medical facilities very

soon,' Chamberlain went on, 'within forty-eight hours all of us may be dead.'

Jennifer was stunned. She had been told a billion people might die, but she hadn't thought yet of all the tangible flesh and blood aboard the train.

'Maybe,' she heard Mackenzie say on the phone, 'but not certainly ... I said we have alternatives.'

'And we're supposed to place our lives in your hands,' Chamberlain replied, his voice rising to a shout. 'Why don't you just stop this train and put us into proper quarantine where we belong?'

'We will ... When you reach your destination.'

'Where in hell are you dragging us?'

Mackenzie exchanged a quick look with one of his aides, who shook his head no.

'You will be informed,' he told Chamberlain, 'I promise. ... What I ask is your cooperation. It will not be easy to keep twelve hundred frightened people under control.'

Chamberlain's jaw tightened. 'I will do everything I can for the safety of these passengers. But if I survive this journey, Mackenzie, *you* will have to answer for every move you make!'

Jennifer's eyes met his.

Elena stared at Mackenzie. He looked worried. She understood that Chamberlain's warning had found its mark. The words 'top secret' rang in her injured ear. She wondered how many people on that train were already feeling sick.

Kaplan felt the air in his compartment growing foul. He stepped into the corridor and adjusted the internal ventilation system control marked: 'Turn knob for fresh air.'

The mother with the infant who had played with Oscar stood nearby. The baby was crying uncontrollably, and the mother, rocking him in her arms and trying to soothe him with soft sounds, could do nothing to quiet her child. She looked at Kaplan and shrugged helplessly.

'Let me hold him,' said Kaplan gently. 'In my time I have put many people to sleep.'

The mother smiled and handed him the infant gratefully. But the change did not avail. Kaplan cradled the child tenderly.

'Shh ... shhh ... *mein Kind*,' he whispered softly, then looking at the mother, he said, 'He feels hot.'

She shook her head anxiously. 'He was shivering a while ago ... We have to go all the way to Amsterdam. I don't know what to do.'

Kaplan wiped some perspiration from the infant's brow.

'He'll be all right,' he said.

The baby cried painfully, but when Kaplan accidentally shielded his eyes from the bright lights overhead, it brought a small measure of relief. The child's tongue seemed unusually large to his mother.

*

At the end of a corridor in first class, the priest stood by the little window set into the door. He turned in every direction to be certain he was alone. His eyes were laced with fear. He carried his small suitcase. He lowered the window and leaned out, looking towards the head of the train.

Outside, the light was failing, evening coming on. The train was nearing Maubeuge station in the north of France. The one-platform station itself was deserted, except for two men, who peered down the empty track, waiting for the Transcontinental Express. One of the men wore tinted glasses; the other was dressed like a priest.

Four armed police came on to the platform, taking up equidistant positions. The two men exchanged alarmed glances.

The air was chill, and vapour poured from their nostrils. The train's approach could be heard but not yet seen. They glanced at the police, who seemed as concentrated on the train's imminent arrival as they.

A whistle from the train blasted a succession of short sounds, giving the standard warning to clear the track. The police drew their guns. The two men began to back away towards a waiting car.

At last the train appeared. It tore past the platform, its whistle screaming long. The men suddenly caught sight of the priest leaning from the open window, terrorstricken.

The police saw him, too, and began waving him back inside. The priest shouted to the men, throwing up his arms in utter despair.

'They're not stopping anywhere!'

The train roared through and was gone. The police put their guns away and left the station. The two men stared at one another.

'Don't worry,' said the man in tinted glasses. 'He's good. Good . . . and scared. He'll find a way to get off.'

On the train, the priest went into the toilet and locked it. He was sweating profusely. He opened his cassock. His waist was girded with two thick belts securing literally hundreds of glassine packets containing a cache of drugs worth near four hundred thousand dollars. He opened one of them and sniffed hard, closing his eyes for a moment or two.

From his small suitcase, he withdrew a black Webley .45 automatic, and wedged the weapon in one of his belts.

*

A microscopic view of a living Pasteurella pestis bacillus magnified 75,000 times flickered on a closed-circuit television screen in Dr Gregorovius Hoffmann's laboratory on a lower floor of the Milestone complex. The organism was in the process of reproduction, the single rod-shaped cell becoming two. A digital clock at the bottom of the screen kept track of the process's elapsed time. It read fifteen minutes, while the seconds and tenths of seconds flashed.

The cellular rod was elongated, constricted at the centre, and a thick, transparent cross-wall was rapidly taking shape just prior to the moment of separation.

'This sample of the infective agent,' Hoffmann was saying to Mackenzie and Elena, 'was, of course, taken from the dog.'

Hoffmann, wearing a large red rose pinned to his white coat, pressed a button and the image of Oscar, being attended by a medical team, appeared on a series of small television screens.

'There he is,' said Hoffmann professorially. 'Still active, but, of course, not very healthy.'

Mackenzie cringed every time Hoffmann said 'of course'.

'There can be no doubt,' the German went on. 'This is the 3XP variant of Pasteurella pestis ... resistant to sulfonamides, champherical, all the mycins, penicillin and every other known antibiotic.' He suddenly grew defensive. 'We do have an antiserum, of course ... but the results have been poor.'

The three of them stared with fascination at the micrograph, as the creature divided.

'It's like being present at a birth,' Elena said.

Mackenzie smirked. 'A devil's birth.'

The clock stopped at 15 minutes, 57.8 seconds. The division process of the new bacilli began again, but the clock remained inert.

'A most remarkable doubling time!' Hoffmann exclaimed,

calculating and muttering to himself. 'The individual variant is forming colonies of a million offspring in less than six hours. A million colonies in twelve hours ... then a million million.' He checked himself from being carried away by his enthusiasm, which he had learned from experience was not always understood by others. 'Of course, it is only a matter of time before we discover an effective drug.'

Mackenzie was irked. 'And only a matter of time before it discovers how to resist the new drug.'

'Of course,' Hoffmann replied. He was hurt.

*

Night had fallen. The lights along the railroad tracks rocketed past the Transcontinental Express. Chamberlain stared out the window of his compartment, lost in thought. Jennifer sat across the room, an open camera in her lap, loading it with film.

They had taken supper together in the dining car, and for the past few hours or so a nervous calm had settled on the train as the passengers had filled their stomachs and wandered off in search of the escape offerings of sleep. Everyone had been advised by the conductors, who were unwittingly conveying what in reality was a Milestone cover story, the half-truth that there would be no stops during the night, nor, for that matter, until the train arrived at Copenhagen, at 2.15 p.m. the following afternoon.

The reason given – in which there was no truth whatsoever – was that the United States had declared a worldwide military alert because of 'trouble in the Middle East'. This 'explanation' had aroused much grumbling, but in the end, though no such news could yet be heard on any of the many portable radios on board, it had been more or less universally accepted. In the first place, the 'Middle East crisis' posed no conceivable immediate threat to the passengers themselves, and secondly, the majority of them were going at least as far as Copenhagen. For this group, the thought of a non-stop journey promised an actual improvement, in spite of the world's woes, and for the others, they could do nothing for now but bear with it – *because* of the world's woes.

At dinner Chamberlain and Jennifer had managed to avoid the matter at hand, talking of everything but. He told her about growing up a loner in Placitas, walking eight miles each day back and forth to school, riding Appaloosa horses in the foothills of the Sandias, and dreaming of the prehistoric men who had lived in the caves he himself had explored. He spoke about his children, the older boy at Harvard, the younger at Andover, where he lived with his mother and stepfather – a musicologist – 'a real nice guy', who, he conceded, was far more right for his ex-wife than he had ever been, or could be.

She recalled her youth in Terre Haute, playing 'doctor' with the boy next door, and an alcoholic father she could not remember having ever seen. She did not speak of the painter; he said nothing of Dr Hellquist. They drank a second bottle of wine and joked about the manner of their meeting, about the self-important steward, and then she told the story about Alfred, the bridegroom, going 'all the way'. And when they had run out of words, he had needlessly excused his silence, straining for *bons mots* and saying finally that he was not much good at social intercourse: when she replied that that was the only kind of intercourse she abhorred, he felt eminently comfortable and the silence between them expressed a deep content.

They had gone back to his compartment, sat apart in the dim blue glow of the inextinguishable nightlight which was fixed in the wall, and had passed at least one mute hour more together in this way. Now she looked up at him, studied his face for a while, then broke the silence.

'Are we really going to die?' There was no fear, only curi-osity, in her voice and Chamberlain's reply was equally de-tached.

'He said the bug was drug-resistant. That leaves us pretty much on our bodies' own defences.' He spoke slowly, thoughtfully, and she knew each word had heuristic mean-ing, yet he was not applying the gratuitous oral therapy with which doctors patronize their patients. 'Some of us will have a kind of natural immunity, I guess. Then, a few people are going to get sick, but recover. A very few. The rest will die ... All in all, I'd say the chances against us are about twenty to one. And—'

He looked at her for a moment, gauging whether to add his last words, deciding finally that she would want him to.

'... a lot more against you and me. We've had a big dose of exposure.'

'Mackenzie said he had alternatives,' Jennifer retorted.

Chamberlain was sceptical. 'When you have something to sell, you advertise.'

Jennifer searched his eyes. She spoke hesitantly, reser-vedly.

'You're not an altogether mediocre man, Dr Chamberlain.'

'Coming from you, Miss Saint, I'd say that was a compli-ment.'

'Compliments are like flowers. There's not much around in the winter.'

Chamberlain remembered a line from Byron. He won-dered if she would laugh if he were to repeat it. ' "Winter is the mother of spring",' he said, somewhat awkwardly.

' "A mile in winter is two",' she said, plucking a counter-poise line, from where she did not know. 'Some hearts can't take the strain,' she added on her own. 'They don't last till April.'

'Hearts can be mended. I've fixed a few myself.'

'Not when they've been torn in two.'

Chamberlain conceded gracefully. He watched her anguished face.

'Afraid?' he asked with tenderness.

'You're scared but you don't know why,' she said, forcing a brave smile. 'You only know that something bad's going to happen . . . but you don't know what. Ever had the feeling?'

Chamberlain nodded respectfully. 'You've been doing a lot of feeling, Miss Saint. And that's a compliment.'

She bowed her head appreciatively. 'Thanks for the compliment, medic.'

He grew intense. 'A woman who really hurt me once, used to call me "medic" . . . a long time ago.' He took a step closer to her. 'Jonathan's my name.'

With a quaint sort of shyness, she replied, 'Jennifer. A few hurts . . . lots of disappointments.'

She extended her hand. He took it in his, shaking it like a gentleman. Her hand was smaller, softer, than it had seemed when he had helped her board the train.

'Pleased to meet you, Jennifer.'

Their hands remained together. Her eyes sought his. They met.

'Jonathan,' she said, 'I hope we don't die.'

*

'The 3XP variant is spread by aerogenic droplet transmission,' Hoffmann was telling Mackenzie and Elena – something they had already known for quite some time. 'That means coughs, sneezes and ordinary breathing. It causes not bubonic but *pneumonic* plague – invariably much more severe, much more fatal.'

Elena sensed Mackenzie's irritation. She tried to get at what they were really after.

'Doctor, when will the people on the train start getting sick?'

'Considering virulence, the extraordinary rate of reproduction, and, of course, the crowded conditions, I would say, that in a normal adult, symptoms such as shivering, vomiting, splitting headache, giddiness, intolerance to light, and, of course—'

'Doctor!' Mackenzie demanded impatiently.

Hoffmann would not allow himself to be intimidated. In the Milestone infrastructure, at least in his own laboratory, he was entitled to deference of no smaller magnitude than Mackenzie's, and deference had to be defended. He continued as if Mackenzie had not spoken at all.

'...tongue swelling, should appear within twelve hours after exposure, with death occurring in the majority of cases twenty-four to forty-eight hours later ... It is of course a very potent—'

'Thank you, doctor,' Mackenzie interrupted. He began to leave, Elena following.

Hoffmann was furious, unnerved. He called after Mackenzie. 'We are working on the serum around the clock, of course.'

Mackenzie turned and nodded politely. 'Of course.'

Then he went out the door.

He sent Elena, if not to sleep, to try to get some rest, and when she advised him to do the same, he nodded placatingly. But he went directly to the Milestone Command Centre with what was now the biggest problem pressing on his mind.

Upstairs, he waited at the telephone, expecting a call from a distant capital.

Saturday

midnight to noon

11 midnight

Jennifer, in her own compartment, sat before a mirror, preparing for bed. Her hair draped loosely around her shoulders as she combed it out. She wore something sheer and clingy, which caressed her sybarite body.

The Jennifer who had climbed aboard that train twelve hours earlier like a hound at the heels of a cur seemed now a preening cat. She had never been one for powder and paint, but she perfumed her body lightly with a neroli scent she had seen women in Thailand use, and she tried to make her hair fall in a very special way.

When at last she felt right, she climbed into bed and waited, first nervously, then, after a while, impatiently. Finally, she got up and put her ear to the wall adjoining Chamberlain's compartment. She listened, but heard nothing. She was about to knock, but she stopped herself, wondering whether she should.

Chamberlain was at a writing table, busily engaged in making a written account of everything that had happened thus far. A cigarette dangled from his lips, his eyes smarting from the smoke. His collar opened, his sleeves rolled back, he was totally immersed in what he was doing.

His pen scratched. His handwriting was unusually legible, for which he never failed to be chided by fellow doctors and patients alike. He wrote: 'One can only guess what effect sealing the train might have. I, myself . . .'

He looked up from his writing, feeling restive, chilled. He rose and moved to the wall, Jennifer's wall. His hand went up to knock, but it dropped before he could bring himself to it, and he returned to his writing.

Jennifer stepped away from the wall and wandered around the room melancholically for a moment. She crawled back into bed, brooding.

'Fuck it!' she muttered, and rolled and curled to her sleeping posture.

But sleep eluded her. She felt only that vague anxiety she had spoken to Chamberlain about, and a longing that demanded fulfilment. She suddenly leaped up and when her naked feet touched the floor, she ran with abandon to her man. She opened her compartment door. Chamberlain was already there. He seemed himself to have been running. They looked at one another. They plunged into each other's arms, turning, holding each other tightly. Jennifer kicked the door closed. There were no words, only passion rising, cascading, lighting every facet of a gem.

*

Some time after four a.m. that morning, Mackenzie burst into the Milestone Command Centre, nailing the attention of everyone awake and startling a few of the Commission members and personnel who had fallen into fitful sleep in the lull.

'The problem,' he announced loudly, 'has been resolved.'

All eyes were questioning, following him as he went to the wall screen and signalled to the communications panel – a gesture which brought a map of Europe on the screen. The question hung in the air like a vapour trail. Which problem had he meant? *The* problem?

'The quarantine site,' he explained.

He turned to the map, missing Elena's sleepy reaction of disappointment and Dr Hoffmann's hostile eyes.

'It wasn't easy,' Mackenzie said. 'Even getting transit through France and Belgium required an ... "inventive" approach. But the final location is ideal.' He turned back to the group. He felt a strange power over everyone, for he was alert, overstimulated perhaps, but in exquisite command of his senses. 'Siberia?' he asked rhetorically. 'Yes, that would have been better, strategically speaking. But the distance is prohibitive, and the Russians' wide-gauge track would have complicated matters endlessly.'

'Where do we go, Mackenzie?' Hoffmann cried out, calculatingly. Now it was his turn to be interruptive, impatient.

Mackenzie signalled again, and the wall screen map changed: Poland. He pointed to the south-east quadrant.

'Here,' he said. 'A virtual desert. Yet, with ample rail lines and communications. A complex of abandoned buildings in the sub-Carpathian basin.' His voice dropped. 'The remains,' he added slowly, disturbedly, 'of a group of Nazi concentration camps.'

Elena was appalled, but Hoffmann, the German, was livid. He fumed.

'But Milestone is a humanitarian effort!' Elena pleaded. 'How can we associate ourselves with a ... a—' she trailed off, unable to even say it.

'Where else can we go?' Mackenzie reasoned. 'The Vélodrome d'Hiver in Paris? The Nazis used that, too. The Colosseum in Rome? Europe is the most densely populated continent of the world. It was either the Polish plains or the steppelands of the USSR. We chose the closer.'

Hoffmann's outrage exploded. 'We cannot send twelve hundred people to such a place! I am certain that if my government knew, it would lodge the severest protest!'

'I'm sure,' Mackenzie said wryly. 'But neither can we add two long days to their journey.' He grew strong. 'And for what? Instead of old Nazi camps, we get old Stalinist camps!'

Hoffmann hardened. He was bitter, sarcastic. 'You think of everything, don't you, Mackenzie?'

Mackenzie did not respond to this. He seemed troubled, though, as if something he had *not* thought of were preying on his mind. He took hold of himself, and picked up a sheaf of papers.

'Now,' he said, 'we seal the train.'

The overhead clock read 4.40. In that part of the world, in that time of the year, the break of day was near.

12 4.47 am

During the night the train had passed through Belgium and most of the Netherlands, following its regular course to Copenhagen and then on to Stockholm via the boat train. Shortly before four a.m., however, when permission had been granted by the Warsaw government to establish a quarantine site near the Janow Station in south-eastern Poland, the Milestone computers had plotted a provisional optimum route to the new destination, and the Transcontinental Express was detoured at exactly 3.59 a.m.

Contingent upon the Polish decision had been the approval of the West Germans to provide the facilities and equipment for the sealing operations. The Dutch had politely refused, claiming a lack of personnel and supplies, but since the train had been in the territory of the Netherlands at the time of the detour, they had cooperated with the Germans in providing easy access, particularly at the Dutch-German frontier, to the sealing point: an immense tract of open flatland in the Ruhr Valley, near Kleve Station on the German side of the border, somewhat south of the fifty-second parallel.

The Transcontinental Express, waved on without stopping by the frontier police, crossed that border now. It was only fifteen minutes or so from Kleve.

At the sealing point, the first light of dawn gave grey form to the empty tracks running east and west. All was stillness, except for the birds.

The sky was clear, and as the sun's messengers of daylight

began to peek over the horizon, the morning calm was ruptured by the roar of a convoy of heavy trucks, some bearing military insignia, others the symbol of the Red Cross.

The convoy began to flank the rails and as each truck reached this objective it drew to a halt. Soldiers in full combat dress leaped from the vans and proceeded to unload welding apparatus, acetylene and oxygen tanks, long metal tubing, and a variety of other equipment and materials. They worked noisily. The growling engines, the clang of iron falling, and the barking of commands had in a matter of moments transformed the quiet of dawn into a mighty din.

That this would happen had been foreseen by Mackenzie, and the timing of the operation had not been fortuitous. He had known that when the train arrived at the sealing point, the confusion would have passed, and at that early hour of the morning most of the people on board would be asleep. Indeed, he had designed the operation to be carried out while the passengers slept to present them with a *fait accompli*, avoiding its fear-provoking aspects as much as was humanly possible. In this regard, he had decided that the windows on the compartment side of the train would at the moment of arrival be immediately painted black. It would be best, he had thought, that if passengers did awake they would be unable to see too much of the operations, which would be visible only on that flank of the train. In this way, he had not had to deprive them entirely of natural light and the view from at least the corridor side of the train, especially since almost all stations between Kleve and Janow were on the painted side, reducing to an acceptable minimum 'untoward' visual communication with people outside.

Already a measure of calm had been restored at the sealing flat, and the train was still some minutes away. All of the soldiers and specialized personnel had come down off the trucks, the motors were spent, and hardly anyone had any thing more to say. They had but to wait. The only movement now was among several squads of armed troops taking up strategic positions to assure that order would prevail.

*

Day was rolling in from the east, but almost everyone on the Transcontinental Express was asleep, even the engineer, for the young fireman was at the controls, piloting the train on a line with the rising sun.

Kaplan slept restlessly, sitting, leaning, and squirming for a posture of comfort. He murmured. He spoke in a language no one on the train had heard him use before: Polish. He said something loud and angry. This awakened him momentarily, but he merely grinned through bleary eyes at no one in particular, and drifted off again. The train began to slow.

Ginger and Parsons were asleep clutched in one another's arms on the narrow bed, but suddenly Parsons opened his eyes wide, slipped undisturbingly from Ginger's limp embrace, and getting to his feet, he began his morning round of gymnastics.

By now the train had arrived at the sealing point, and flagged by a man in white, it crept to a fixed point on the rails.

Parsons had not done more than two or three deep knee-bends, when his eyes, coming up to the level of the window, were transfixed. What looked to him like an entire army stood in wait for the train to halt. The advance troops were dressed in white, in the eagle-like protective costume. They began to approach the train slowly, the crown of the morning sun casting purple shadows on the plain.

'Ho – ly shittt!' Parsons muttered to himself.

Almost imperceptibly, the train came to a complete stop and immediately a man in white appeared as if from nowhere framed in Parsons' window. The two men on either side of the glass stared at one another for an instant, each startled by the other. But the man outside, who was carrying a bucket of tar, suddenly splashed the window and began to paint it black, enclosing Parsons in renewed darkness.

Outside, the same procedure was unfolding across the entire north flank of the train, while another team, using a plastic foam material sprayed from an aerosol cylinder, performed the actual sealing. They closed every juncture in the frames of the windows, the doors, and the linkages from car to car. Like white locusts devouring their prey they swarmed over the train while the passengers slept.

Even the sick baby had found sleep in the arms of his mother. The priest, too, was asleep, but one hand clutched the part of his robe that covered his gun. The American students slept hard, except for Susan, who was extremely fitful. Yassan was in a coma. He was white. His head rolled slowly from side to side.

More and more passengers, however, were coming out of sleep. Alfred was 'going all the way', having performed the feat for a number of times which he at least believed had established a wedding-night record worthy of Guinness.

Jennifer was wide awake, trying for the past few minutes to photograph whatever she could before her window would be painted black. Less dressed than she had been when Chamberlain had taken her in his arms, she was wrapped in a sheet secured by the weight of the camera strapped around her, and she moved from one difficult position to another, trying for maximum photographic coverage.

Chamberlain was in Jennifer's bathroom, unaware of what was taking place outside. When he came out, drying his face with a towel, he stared at Jennifer, trying to determine what she was up to. Whatever it was, the movement of her body in the haphazardly arranged bedsheet was captivating.

'You're beautiful,' he said.

She had felt his eyes upon her, but there was not a moment for a word of explanation, nor any need, since the window was suddenly splattered with tar and one man outside began to paint, while another sprayed the seal.

Chamberlain bolted to the window. He tried to lower it, but one of the men held it shut driving his brush-handle upward, as the sealer completed his work. There was a brief struggle to force the window, but Chamberlain could not overcome the strength of the two men and the quick-drying sealing compound.

Jennifer, who had been photographing the entire episode, finally stopped Chamberlain.

'No use behaving like caged animals,' she said. 'They haven't got to all the windows yet.' She handed him a small tape recorder. 'Here, you want a record, don't you? Take notes.'

Chamberlain took the machine and nodded. Jennifer dropped the sheet from around her naked body and began to dress hurriedly. Chamberlain, for all his patch-quilt trip through life, was still the boy from the Sandia foothills and he felt it behoved him to perform the formal, gentlemanly gesture.

'I'll wait outside,' he said.

Jennifer was worming her head through a turtleneck, coming up messy but smiling.

'I thought I told you to take notes,' she scolded, adding a bottomless punctuation.

*

On the roof of the train a shower of sparks burst in the morning air as two pieces of metal were being fused together. Two men in white, wearing welding masks over their eagle-like hoods, worked on the security car that had been attached before the bypass of Basel. The car had been opened and the men inside were filing out rapidly and being urged to put as much distance as possible between them and the train, since they were not wearing any protective clothing.

At the same time, a squad of men in white loaded tanks of oxygen on board, while still another group approached the train, hauling generator equipment, lengths of piping, electric cable and tools.

Three freight cars were being pushed down the track to be added to the rear of the train. One of them was to be used to carry drinking water, medicines, food, and fuel for the new diesel engine which was to replace the electric locomotive. The diesel was needed because of the lack of electrification between the Ostrava Crescent and Janow Station. At the moment it was being fitted down track with an access diaphragm.

The second freight car was a kind of hastily put together hospital wagon with medical personnel already inside. An entire section of this car had been stocked with about one hundred steel containers measuring eighteen inches wide by eighteen inches deep by six feet long.

The third car – first in the coupling order – was to contain a new escort of thirty-six men wearing the protective gear. At the moment, they assembled outside waiting to board. They stood amid wooden crates of ammunition, adjusting their protective clothing and hoods in anticipation of the order to mount the train. They carried sub-machine guns and flamethrowers.

*

Mackenzie leaned over a scale model of the Transcontinental Express briefing the others on the details of the operation now underway.

'Once sealed ...' he was saying, realizing how weary were his listeners. He himself felt lucid and strong. '... the train will be given a pressurized atmosphere similar to that of commercial aircraft, though considerably lower. It will circulate bacterially-filtered fresh air at the standard rate of ten cubic feet per minute per person.'

He indicated the points on the model at which the internal ventilation system would be modified.

'This atmosphere, however, will be of high oxygen content. It involves a substantial risk. But as an increasing number of passengers will be taken ill, suffering acute cardio-respiratory stress, it is a risk worth taking, and every precaution will be observed.'

There was scarce reaction from the others. Mackenzie felt he was merely going through the motions, yet this rehearsal of his previous planning and decisions seemed valuable to him for his own sake.

'Some six miles of zinc tubing are being installed,' he went on, trying to visualize what was happening at Kleve, 'not only for the air supply system, but also for plumbing – to remove for later destruction, all human wastes which would normally be released on the tracks.'

Mackenzie brought up on the scale model the three additional cars to be added to the train, and he explained their functions.

'Our security contingent will be doubled,' he said finally, 'an internationalized police force, which will have access to the entire train. This will assure an orderly passage.'

He looked at the faces around him: tired, riddled with uncertainty. He, too, began to feel the same.

13 5.45 am

Kaplan came out of the toilet carrying a plastic bag and adjusting his fly. He was clean-shaven, morning fresh, and bright-eyed. For him, it was just another day, another dollar.

Standing at the head of the corridor, he became aware that the window on the right, in which the break of day was clearly visible, stood in sharp contrast to the one on the left, which was pitch black. He looked at one, then the other and repeated the motion more than once. A perplexed look grew in his face, but finally he gave up, commenting in his best French accent.

'Ze night, *messieurs, mesdames*,' he announced to no one but himself, 'she is stuck to ze window.'

He began to walk down the corridor, but was almost thrown from his feet as Jennifer and Chamberlain jostled him, running fast on their way to the rear of the train. After they had gone, he straightened himself, dusted his sleeve, and watched them disappear into the next car. Only then did he shake a mock angry fist at them, his humour apparently indomitable as he walked back to his second-class compartment with a bouncy step.

*

In her darkened first-class compartment, little Catherine, while everyone else still slept, drew aside the night curtains on the door for a look into the corridor. She saw the unpainted side of the train and like Kaplan tried to determine why the window on the compartment side was black while the other showed the sky turning blue.

Her eyes went around the room at the sleeping passengers and came to rest on the priest. His head nodded, but he suddenly awoke with a start.

'Why is it still dark on this side?' Catherine asked him abruptly.

The priest looked at her oddly, then crossed his lips with his fingers for her to be quiet. Instead, Catherine pulled back the curtains so that he could see for himself.

'See?' she said raising her voice challengingly. 'I told you!'

The others in the compartment stirred, as the priest

looked with astonishment. He lurched to the curtained door and looked outside to confirm what the girl was showing him. Catherine was quite triumphant.

'I *told* you.'

The priest jumped to his feet and tried to lift the painted window. It would not budge. He pounded on it in an attempt to loosen it, but to no avail.

By now everyone in the compartment had been awakened if by nothing else by the loud banging on the window, and they looked around questioningly, dazedly. No one moved as they watched the priest go to the unpainted window in the corridor and try that one. Again, in spite of a violent effort, he was without success.

Passengers from every compartment seemed suddenly to be on their feet trying themselves to open the windows on both sides of the train. The priest moved down the corridor continually testing the windows. As he made his way towards the toilet at the corridor's end, he heard shouting from every direction.

'What's wrong *now*?'

'This is a nightmare!'

'Let us out of here!'

The priest locked himself in the toilet. He tried the small frosted window in there. No luck. He drew his gun from beneath his cassock and began to hammer the butt against the black painted glass. It was quite resistant, but after a few powerful blows, it cracked, leaving a small round hole with a diameter about as large as that of the handle of the gun. The priest, removing with his hand the shatterproof glass splinter by splinter, began to enlarge the opening.

He did not get it wider than a man's fist, however, when the hole framed a hooded figure in white, pointing a sub-machine gun between his eyes.

'Get back!'

The priest retreated in fear.

Outside, the guard motioned to others near him to replace the broken window. They immediately went to a stockpile of all sorts of train windows, which had been brought for this eventuality. The damage was soon enough repaired.

*

At the very end of the train, Jennifer had found a position from which she could photograph at least some of what was taking place outside. She could see the welding work being done on the security car, and from the window set into the door between the end of the train and the security car – which had not been sealed since it would lie within the access diaphragm in preparation – she could lean out and see the operational side of the train.

Moving cautiously to avoid being detected, she recorded as much as she could on film.

*

Chamberlain, wearing only a surgical mask for protection, was examining Yassan with his stethoscope. The young man's heart was remarkably strong, but he had clearly suffered severe pulmonary infarction and it seemed only a matter of time before his embolismic lungs would give way, bringing on death by asphyxiation.

He lifted Yassan's head and tried to give him some water, but he was comatose and it was dangerous for Chamberlain to persist. Instead, he merely moistened Yassan's dry, cracked lips.

*

The order for the new escort to board was given by an officer with captain's bars pinned to his white costume. The armed men moved swiftly, efficiently. They seemed disciplined. They wore the blue armband of the United Nations, but, in fact, they were members of a crack battalion of the West German army.

Jennifer, realizing she was in danger of being seen now, took a few last shots of the police mounting the security car and made a fast retreat. She could hear the doors of the newly attached cars being slammed shut.

14 6.10 am

The priest elbowed through a corridor choked with passengers mumbling to one another, looking for someone in authority to alleviate their total ignorance of what was going on. Outside, the sun had risen above the distant trees. The corridor was alive with brilliant light, though the compartments lay in artificial darkness.

The priest was trying to get back to his place on the train, when a surprised voice in the crowd shouted to look out the window. Like everyone else, he turned.

Behind discs and shafts of morning sunlight spilling into the passengers' eyes, a white Red Cross truck could be seen climbing a nearby grassy knoll in the otherwise flat and empty countryside. On its roof were two large loudspeakers. The truck came to a halt about fifty yards from the train and slowly manoeuvred into a position where the loudspeakers faced the passengers like two bulging eyes looking out from the sun.

No one awake was in his seat, every eye was fixed on the truck with the reassuring cross. The loudspeakers crackled, like the clearing of a great throat. Then they spoke. It seemed the voice of God.

'Attention! Attention, please! This announcement will be made in English, German, French and Italian, *one time only*! So please pay careful attention! ... *Achtung! ... Achtung!...*'

The loudspeakers continued the introductory announcement in the other three languages. Jennifer, who had caught up with Chamberlain, stood with him at a window while he recorded the announcement on tape. They were silent, close to one another. Ginger and Parsons were nearby. She seemed half-asleep and wore a sort of veil to cover her unmade-up face. Parsons loosened his muscles.

When the four-language introduction ended, there were several moments of total silence. The priest had edged his way to a position just outside his own compartment. He pressed his hand against his gun. He stood next to Mrs Chadwick and Catherine.

'Ladies and gentlemen,' the loudspeakers began again, 'you have been exposed to a highly communicable, infectious disease...'

On the words, 'infectious disease', the mother of the sick baby was stabbed with fear, which, perhaps to a lesser extent, was the general reaction among most but not all the passengers. Ginger, for example, unleashed a theatrical gesture of disbelief, Mrs Chadwick seemed terribly annoyed, and Kaplan was simply unimpressed.

The loudspeakers continued. The sun, a little higher than before, relieved some of the tension in the people's eyes.

'It is necessary that you be transported to a quarantine site,' said the voice, 'a health camp, where you will be kept under medical observation for twenty-one days.'

The priest was thunderstruck and broke out into a sweat. His eyes shifted in every direction, but came back continually to Catherine.

Catherine herself was bored, standing around hearing words whose import she could not fully comprehend, though she tried now and then to seem serious and attentive. She paid more mind to the grumbling which at that moment was going around her.

'Must be that Arab-looking kid they carried through the train yesterday,' someone standing near Mrs Chadwick said to her.

'Why don't they just take him off?' Mrs Chadwick asked. 'I really must get back to England.'

'Why don't they just *throw* him off?' another passenger intervened. 'I'm gonna miss a charter flight!'

Most of this went over Catherine's head, but she distinctly heard the word 'Arab' being whispered among many of the passengers.

The loudspeakers continued.

'All modern health care will be provided free of charge: doctors, medicines, every possible convenience.'

Jennifer thought of the steel containers she had seen and photographed. She frowned.

'You are about to depart on a fourteen-hour, non-stop journey to the health camp.'

The old woman going to her son's funeral wailed, 'My children ... they won't know where ...'

Other passengers looked at her, showing the same concern about their families.

'Your names will be collected,' the loudspeakers intoned. 'Your families notified.'

Some passengers were already beginning to feel relieved. Kaplan seemed almost pleased. Not a bad deal. A chance to sell off all his wares.

'The following lifesaving measures *must* be observed!' said the speakers emphatically. 'One. Obey all orders of the security police now boarding your train ...'

The white-clad troop began taking up their positions in the crowded corridors. Each of them was armed, their bodies shrouded from head to foot in the protective costume.

This came as a total shock to the passengers, who only now began to fully realize, in seeing how the guards had to protect themselves from them, how infectious the disease must be. The guards moved among them commandingly, but were not in any way violent or even discourteous, which had the effect of dampening the initial reaction.

'Panic must be avoided. No breach of discipline will be tolerated. Two. The train has been hermetically sealed. Any attempt to break this seal will be stopped by force...'

The new situation was taking shape for the priest, who knew he would have to act before whatever chances he had might be lost. Standing directly beside Catherine, he moved slightly to block the entrance to his compartment. With an eye on the security police, slowly, with great circumspection, he slid his gun from his belt into his hand, concealing it in the loose sleeve of his cassock.

'Three. Smoking is an extreme fire hazard...'

Though the high oxygen air supply had not yet been turned on, some passengers who were smoking immediately crushed their cigarettes.

'When the train starts,' the announcement went on, 'no smoking will be permitted.'

The passengers who had extinguished their cigarettes lit up anew for one last smoke.

'All matches, cigarette lighters and electric appliances of any kind will be collected.'

Kaplan, who had a whole store of cigarette lighters in his pockets, tried to hide them. But he was immediately spotted by a security guard, who motioned to him to turn them over. Kaplan held them out.

'Three for two dollars,' he said hopefully. '*Sechs mark fünfzig.*'

The guard insisted. Kaplan shrugged and handed them to him.

'Four. All incidence of sickness must be reported at once to Dr Jonathan Chamberlain, one of your fellow passengers.'

Chamberlain lifted his eyebrows. This had come as somewhat of a surprise to him.

The mother with the sick baby clutched the infant closer to her and began to sob. The baby breathed irregularly; she shaded him from the harsh light.

'Five. Remain in your own compartment as much as possible. And under no circumstances will you be allowed to leave your car...'

The priest studied the guards at both ends of the corridor closing off all passage.

'Finally, a leaflet containing further details will be distributed. Read this carefully...'

Kaplan, completely relaxed, turned to a very frightened-looking Gunther and tried to placate him.

'So?' he said throwing up his hands nonchalantly. 'What's so terrible? They take us to the health centre, give us the cure. Three weeks' free room and board. Then you go your way, I go mine. *Nicht gefällig?*'

Gunther wrung his hands. He was about to say something, but the loudspeakers came on with some final words.

'Please cooperate. Your own lives are at stake. Your destination is the Janow Station in the south-eastern part of Poland ... We wish you a safe journey.'

The German version of the announcement began immediately. Kaplan suddenly paled. In a seizure of panic, he grabbed Gunther by his jacket lapels and began to shake him violently.

'What did he say!'

Gunther looked at him as if he were mad. He tried to shake himself loose, but Kaplan clung to him desperately.

'He wished us a safe journey,' Gunther replied forcing Kaplan's hands from him.

'No!' Kaplan cried frantically, seizing the man once again. 'The destination! Where? Where?'

'Some place in Poland.'

Kaplan began to shriek hysterically.

'No! ... No! ... I can't! They don't understand! I can't! ... *Ich kann nicht nach Polen gehen!*'

Kaplan weakened his hold on Gunther and simply leaned on him. Gunther pushed him away. Kaplan began to run through the crowd towards the door, crying out insanely.

'I can't go back to Poland! ... Stop the train!'

The train, of course, was stationary, and while like Gunther many were convinced he had suddenly gone berserk, others who had come to know him during the trip, thought he was acting out some kind of clownish prank. They laughed at him, somewhat hesitantly at first, but more insistently as Kaplan continued to rage.

Kaplan worked his way towards the door, shouting in several languages. Some of the merchandise he kept in the lining of his jacket was being torn away as he drilled through the crowd. It fell to the floor where it was crushed underfoot. But this meant nothing to him now as he plunged ahead. The laughing began to fade.

The German version of the announcement rung in his ears and he shouted at the loudspeakers, beating his fists on the windows.

'Ich kann nicht zurück gehen!'

At last he arrived at the door, which was blocked by a security guard. He tried to fight his way past him, but he was no match for his armed opponent. Instead, he turned away and pounded on the door to the next car, weeping openly and slumping to the floor.

'I can't go back,' he sobbed. 'My wife ... my babies ... my poor babies ...'

He broke out into Polish, then murmured unintelligible phrases. No one could any longer believe that he was anything but deadly serious, and the guard, aided by a passenger, lifted Kaplan to his feet and helped him to his compartment. Kaplan's face was bathed in tears as he continually shook his head no. He was led to his seat and he buried his head in his lap. His whole body was wracked violently as he cried without relenting.

The German version of the announcement had just been completed and now the French began.

Jennifer was deep in thought, shaking her head no. She turned to Chamberlain.

'They can't go to Poland ... not to the Janow Station,' she said.

He looked at her inquiringly.

'If I had a map, I could show you.'

'There's one in every compartment,' he replied dubiously.

'Your place, or mine?'

He stared at her. She left. He followed.

*

Mackenzie had been following the Kleve announcements over the Milestone intercom, when Elena came up to him holding a computer printout.

'Looks like we can't get to Janow,' she said enigmatically.

He stared at her sharply, his eyes demanding a speedy clarification.

'The computer ran a routine check on itself and rejected its earlier course-plotting operations. Now it won't let the train proceed beyond the Ostrava Crescent in northern Czechoslovakia. Seems the computer is suffering from an alphanumeric insufficiency in the main memory unit. Needs more data. Books, documents, articles, etcetera. Nobody knows where to get all this material.'

Mackenzie was silent. He despised anthropomorphic references to machines. He had wanted to shout that computers don't suffer – but not at someone who did.

'What do we do?' Elena inquired.

'Ask the computer!' he snapped. '*I'm* only human.'

Elena said nothing, but Mackenzie knew she had understood his plea and that she, like him, was reflecting on its import.

*

The Italian, final version of the announcement was coming to an end.

The priest still stood beside Catherine assessing the situation with darting eyes. It was clear that the train would depart once again.

The general mood was one of being completely in the hands of the gods. A few passengers, attempting to ape the style of the ever-present security guards, had wrapped white handkerchiefs around their nose and mouth in the belief that it might afford them some degree of protection, but most people seemed languid, docile, unburdened in that an apparently knowledgeable and powerful authority had finally taken their misfortunes in hand.

At last, the final repeat of the announcement was completed, and without loss of time or further ceremony, the train began to move again, gaining velocity quite rapidly.

The security troops moved about, checking to see that all cigarettes were extinguished, and the whirr of the ventilating system could be heard building up to operational speed.

The priest looked around him. A guard was nearby, collecting matches. The passengers who had been sharing the priest's compartment, including Mrs Chadwick, were approaching him with the obvious intention of resuming their seats. He stood in their way.

Suddenly, he grabbed Catherine around the neck with one arm and extended the other, stretching it beyond his sleeve to reveal the gun in his hand. There was a gasp full of dread.

Catherine screamed and fought back, kicking and biting the priest. He tightened his hold on her while covering her mouth to suffocate her cries. But she continued to battle him as he dragged her into the empty compartment. He pushed her violently behind him. She fell to the floor, scraping her knees.

He tore away his annoying collar, shouting to the others.

'Back! All of you!' he cried brandishing his gun. 'I didn't learn to use this by pissing in church!'

Everyone retreated, except Mrs Chadwick. She was paralysed in complete disbelief. Profaned. Suddenly she lunged for the priest, screaming hysterically.

'Beast!'

She tried to maul him, her nails digging into his flesh. He could not shake her. He fired the gun. The bullet ripped through her chest. Her eyes frozen in a hideous mixture of ultimate terror and disillusionment, Mrs Chadwick fell dead.

Passengers shrieked. The security guard pushed his way forward, his sub-machine gun at the ready. Catherine, who had got to her feet again, struck the priest below the waist. He doubled up, but put the pistol to her head, forcing her to him.

The guard held his weapon on the priest, who stared into the narrow slits that covered the eyes beneath his white hood.

'You!' he cried to the guard, pressing his gun at Catherine's temple. 'Listen to me carefully! I'm getting off. I want a plane, a pilot, and fuel to fly two thousand miles. Clear?'

The guard nodded, lowering his gun. The priest glanced at his watch.

'You have one hour!'

Digging his fingers into Catherine's face, he pulled her back into the compartment and slid the door shut.

In the corridor, the crowd ringed around Mrs Chadwick's body. Two or three more guards pushed through. They were followed by two white-clad members of the medical personnel, carrying in the manner of stretcher bearers one of the six-foot steel containers that had been placed on board at Kleve.

The guards made room for them. They examined her very briefly to certify death and lowered her lids over the horror-laden stare in her eyes. Then they placed the body in the steel container, sealing the lid with aerosol styrofoam sprayed from a backpack cylinder. The passengers gazed hypnotically.

*

Chamberlain and Jennifer were in his compartment standing at the wall map showing the main railways of continental Europe.

'Whatever route they take,' she said confidently, 'they have to go through the Cracow Gate.' She pointed with facility. 'Which means crossing the Carpathians, more precisely, through the Jablunkov Pass and the range called the Tatra Mountains.'

She touched all these places with equal ease, but Chamberlain looked at her sceptically.

'You get "A" in geography,' he said. 'How about maths? What does it all add up to?'

'One.'

Chamberlain was becoming impatient now. She sailed on further.

'Between the Jablunkov Pass and the Cracow Gate, there's a high altitude crossing in the Tatra range. It's unsafe.'

Chamberlain continued to register doubt, but she did not wait for him to raise any questions, anticipating them and proceeding rapidly now.

'How do I know?' she asked rhetorically. 'Concentration camp stories. I've done loads of them: memorials, anniversaries, state visits ... I've been over that crossing a dozen times – but in an old Toonerville trolley, not a train like this. I was supposed to have done a story on it once for *Life*, but *National Geographic* beat us to it – which didn't help *Life* very much. My story – and theirs – was that if a modern, fully-loaded transcontinental train ever made the run, the crossing might collapse.'

'Might?'

Jennifer nodded, ignoring his persistent incredulity.

'The mountain people have watched it sag for generations. Marked it year by year on one of the supports – twenty-five inches since 1892. In the Tatras, they call it the *Kasan-druv Prejezd* – the Cassandra Crossing.'

Chamberlain was struck by this. He recalled an old Pueblo legend that had haunted his boyhood, which he later discovered was an almost perfect analogue of the Cassandra myth. He had never gone much for the Greek stories, but something somewhere inside him still believed the Pueblos.

'Cassandra had the gift of prophecy,' he said as if to himself, 'and the curse of never to be believed.'

'Like me,' said Jennifer nodding. 'Right now. Unless someone believes me.'

'Only dreamers will believe you.'

'Do you?'

Chamberlain surveyed her face, her eyes. He had no ready answer.

*

In a second-class compartment a hand reached up and pulled the red handle labelled in four languages, 'Emergency Brake – Pull Downward Sharply in Case of Danger – Penalties for Abuse'.

Nothing happened. It was Kaplan's hand. He appeared distraught, despondent. He pulled the handle again and again with increasing fury. The other passengers tried to stop him. Finally, he fell back into his seat, resting his head on his knees.

*

In the enginer's cab, the emergency handle light glowed red on the control panel. The engineer switched it off, nodding to the fireman to go back for a look. He opened the door of the cab. Outside were four security guards with sub-machine guns. They looked at him questioningly, ready to be of service. Reassured, the fireman tried to appear authoritative, motioning to them to carry on.

16 8.00 am

Mackenzie, showing signs of having gone too long without sleep, was on the radio-telephone, shouting into the microphone. Hoffmann, who seemed rather haggard, too, but with somewhat greater self-control, was beside him.

'Hostage or no hostage,' Mackenzie cried, 'no one gets off that train, captain!'

In the communications car, the security guard wearing two gold bars of leadership replied to Mackenzie.

'But, sir, he has threatened to kill the little girl within the hour.'

Mackenzie listened, struggling for inner strength.

'We won't be intimidated,' he said with finality. 'We'll make one offer only: we'll meet his demands at Janow Station. But there will be no stops between here and the camp!'

He hung up, shaken. Hoffmann tried to be ingratiating.

'I admire your fortitude,' he said with a half-smile. 'The criminal mind must be won by courage ... And a child of that age, of course ... well, she probably won't survive the disease anyway.'

Mackenzie stared deeply into Hoffmann's eyes as rage grew in his own.

'Hoffmann,' he asked icily, 'do you have children?'

'Yes ... but—'

'So do I ... a girl, nine years old.'

He turned and left without waiting for response of any kind. Hoffmann's face hardened.

*

Catherine sat in a corner of her compartment staring at the priest. She seemed angry, not afraid. Determined, not submissive. The priest looked away.

The Transcontinental Express sped eastwards racing through a small station east of Marburg. The platform was empty, except for police who lined the way. When it had passed, a single locomotive moved slowly in its wake. A white spray poured from a series of nozzles fitted to the locomotive, blanketing the tracks with a bactericidal salt of mercury. It looked like snow.

*

Chamberlain had asked to speak with Mackenzie, who had gone off to get some rest. He had insisted that it was urgent that he speak with him at once regardless of any circumstances, and after a grinding bout with the Milestone bureaucracy, he had finally succeeded in having Mackenzie called to the phone. Now, while he waited, he stood with Jennifer, feeling a rush of doubt renewed as he looked into her eyes.

The operator handed him the receiver. Before he began to speak he glanced at Jennifer oddly for a moment. But the timbre of his voice was strong as he talked into the phone.

'Mackenzie, did you ever hear of the Cassandra Crossing?'

Mackenzie was taken aback, but he replied confidently.

'We're already working on it, Chamberlain. Two governments, a task force of engineers, and a million dollars' worth of electronic hardware ... I will let you know. Let us take care of the driving. You take care of the sick.'

Mackenzie hung up, sighing wearily. He wondered if now he might find some rest; worse, if he would ever rest again.

*

The priest, again holding his gun to Catherine's head, stood at the half-open door of the compartment talking to the captain of the security guards.

'All right!' he shouted angrily. 'As far as the camp! But if this is a trick . . .'

He drove the gun viciously into Catherine's temple, forcing her hard against the backrest of the seat in which she had been sitting. Then he slid the door shut.

Infuriated, he dropped into a seat in the corner opposite Catherine, fussed for a while, then looked at her.

Catherine was shivering, but not out of fear. She spoke to him with strange authority.

'You killed Mrs Chadwick. You're not a priest. You're an ogre . . . and ogres always die.'

Her teeth began to chatter violently.

'I'm c-c-cold,' she said.

The priest turned his head away, but a moment later, he looked back at her, and he seemed concerned, frightened. He approached her. She tried to pull away, but he touched her brow with the palm of his hand. She was feverish. Alarmed, he took down Mrs Chadwick's coat from the luggage rack and offered it to Catherine. But her hands quivered uncontrollably and she could not grasp it. He wrapped her in the coat.

'Listen, kid,' he said worriedly, 'don't get sick on me now. . . . Please don't get sick on me.'

He stared at her face. Her complexion was sallow, her lips dry. She breathed heavily through her mouth. Her tongue was coated.

'Please don't get sick on me,' the priest repeated pleadingly.

Catherine's eyes darkened threateningly.

'I will!' she cried. 'I will!'

*

The second-class compartment occupied by the mother and

the baby had been cleared of all the other passengers, and Chamberlain, summoned by a guard, was examining the infant, who showed symptoms very much like Catherine's. In the corridor, people watched fearfully from behind the 'safety' of the glass door.

'I called for you immediately,' the mother said guiltily, her eyes falling for having said something less than the truth.

Chamberlain, sensing this, regarded the mother with a sympathetic look, however, having already made his diagnosis.

'The child must be isolated at once,' he said. 'I'm sorry, you'll have to remain behind.'

The mother gasped. The guard took the baby in his arms and Chamberlain started to leave, but she stopped him.

'But, doctor ... my baby ...' She pointed to her breasts. 'He needs me.'

'He'll have all the proper foods,' he said reassuringly. But he was simply trying to mollify her. He had no idea what arrangements had been made to feed the passengers, though he knew that long ago the dining car had run bare. In any event, he thought as he left the compartment, the baby would be in no condition to retain food of any kind, although the dehydration effect of high fever would make him crave for liquid.

*

Kaplan was in a sweat. He sat trance-like in his seat, his eyes shifting nervously, his hands fidgety.

The other passengers in his compartment had begun to stare at him. They all seemed to be thinking the same thought: that Kaplan had been stricken. Suddenly, one of them got up and left, keeping his distance from Kaplan as he slipped by.

Kaplan looked at him momentarily, then at the others. He bent his head over his knees, and rocked as if in pain. Another passenger left. Then another. In a few moments he was alone. He moved to a seat near the door and drew the curtains.

*

The blinds were drawn in Mackenzie's well-appointed office high above the Milestone complex. The sound of running water echoed in the darkened room. A radio played softly.

Mackenzie turned off the tap and came out from behind a screen, drying himself. Awards, diplomas, paintings and sculpture decorated the office. A child's drawing hung on a wall, and as Mackenzie moved to his desk he stopped and stared at it for a moment or two.

His daughter's name was Melanie and he had not seen her in a year. She had come late in an anaesthetized marriage that had simply endured. At an age he had long ago interred for all time, he had taken a farmer's girl from Winnipeg, that prairie too close to the pole to ever release the cold from human bones. He had brought her to Montreal, where he had studied at McGill. There had been, in the very beginning, romance, joy and even love, but they all too soon were crippled by a psychosis which had climbed upon her back letting up only for brief respites. Those were the years when there had been so much to do, so many marks to be made, but he had nursed her, suffered her, with as much patience as he possessed, through the immutable cycles of sky highs and hellish lows.

One day, when she had no longer been able to call on the extravagant demands on human energy needed to maintain her sickness, she surrendered to a bleak normality, or so it seemed, and Melanie was born. But the child's mother had been worn threadbare, and the years of mental conflagration had not only arrested her development but had rendered her a relic of a useless past. She had gone back to Winnipeg, the child in her arms, vowing never to leave home again. He sent more than enough money every month. He visited whenever time allowed. The child seemed a bright, happy girl, though he knew she sensed the absence of a father she might count on and he worried for the cold that was creeping into her bones. He could feel the ache of winter in his own.

He sat in his leather chair. It was big, roomy and comfortable, the prize of the number one man. There was a soft knock at the door. It opened and Elena looked inside.

'Come in,' he said. 'I'm too agitated to sleep.'

'Shall I get you something?'

Mackenzie shook no and motioned to her to approach him.

'The priest?' he asked anxiously. 'How's the little girl?'

'He accepted,' said Elena, trying to find his eyes in the darkness. 'No problems.'

'For the moment,' he replied dubiously. He tried to relax. He lit a cigarette and leaned back in his chair. But immediately his thoughts turned to other concerns.

'There are weaknesses, Elena,' he said, his eyes focusing at some distant point beyond her. 'We pretend otherwise, but we have lost control ... We lost it the moment we assumed that one group of people could take hold of the fate of another.'

'But people must be protected.'

Mackenzie leaned forward, suddenly alert and vigorous.

'And *we* are their protectors?' he asked. '*God* made this world, leaving men with a brain too powerful for the flesh, too impotent to discover truth.'

'A billion lives may be at stake. You said so yourself. Do we sit back and do nothing?'

'No ... We must do what we have to do – even in the blind ignorance of what the future holds.'

There was silence. He fell back in his chair again. It creaked.

'When I was a boy, Elena,' he said softly now, 'I used to pray every night by the side of my bed. Then I discovered, after a while, that even *I* wasn't listening. So I turned to science ... and there I found, after a while, not Truth and Light, but a new god and new religion. Now I have come full circle. I return to prayer. And my prayer is that what the good men do will outweigh the evil.'

Elena had found his eyes. They closed and he fell off to sleep. His lighted cigarette still burned between his fingers. She removed it and crushed it in an ashtray.

17 9.50 am

'Anybody need a light?'

Tom, the black student, was vaunting a packet of paper matches, wearing a mischievous smile. The others looked at him with no amusement, and Betty berated him.

'You were supposed to turn those in,' she said.

'I was supposed to go to Basel.'

'We're breathing oxygen, Tom.'

'Yeah, "dephlogisticated air" ... That's what they used to call it, man. 'Cause it came from some shit called "phlogiston", which was supposed to be what fire was made of. I know all about science. I used to have a chemistry set.'

He struck one of the matches. It burned in a brilliant white flame, consuming the shaft many times faster than normal. He put a cigarette in his mouth and lit it, but the entire cigarette caught fire with the same white-hot flame. The others all jumped back in a fright. Tom clapped the fire out quickly with the palms of his hands, laughing at their fear.

'Y'see,' he chided, 'they didn't have to say no smoking. Y'can't, man.'

He put the matches in his pocket, patting it as if it contained riches.

A sudden moan filled the compartment. All eyes turned

to Susan. She sat in a corner, trembling, shielding her face from the light.

*

Chamberlain and the steward were hurrying down the crowded corridor of a second-class car.

'He's got it, I'm sure!' said Steward Tickler excitedly. 'He just sits there. Won't answer. Won't move. Won't look at you. And keeps mumbling in some foreign language.'

Chamberlain regarded him suspiciously. These did not sound very much like the symptoms, but his attention was drawn away, for as they walked several passengers intercepted him, shouting pleas:

'Where's the food?'

'My children are hungry!'

'They promised us food and water!'

'I have money; I'll pay double!'

Chamberlain looked at the steward questioningly.

'Tons of food were placed on board, sir,' he said without hesitation. 'Saw it myself.'

Chamberlain felt reassured. They arrived at the compartment of the suspected stricken passenger. The crowd lay back. The curtains were drawn and Chamberlain could not look inside. He knocked. No answer. He tried to slide the door open, but it resisted. Something had been wedged against it.

With assistance from the steward he forced the door, only to be confronted, however, by a man charging the black window with a large Samsonite suitcase. The man, with his back to Chamberlain, smashed up against the glass. There was a loud thud, but the window held.

He wheeled around. It was Kaplan. Chamberlain rushed him, but Kaplan tore himself from his grasp and battered the window again. It cracked and the escape of pressurized air whistled through the glass, ripping away bits and pieces. Frantically, Kaplan began pulling on the slivers of shattered glass to widen the opening, but he succeeded only in cutting his hands and shredding his clothes.

Chamberlain tried to drag him away from the window, but Kaplan, bleeding profusely, fought him. Chamberlain forced him to the floor. Kaplan had cut himself seriously, and blood spouted like a fountain from a vein in his arm.

'Hold him down!' Chamberlain shouted to the steward as he continued to battle with the desperate man. 'He needs a tourniquet!'

But Steward Tickler stood there immobile, afraid to approach Kaplan.

'Do as I say!' Chamberlain cried, realizing the steward's fright. 'He doesn't have it, you fool!'

The steward took a step back. His horror was overwhelming. He slammed the curtained door, disappearing. Chamberlain was left entirely alone with Kaplan, trying to pin him to the floor and stop his bleeding. His blood was being pumped out of his body in a sticky rain that drenched them both.

Suddenly, Kaplan relented. He went limp and looked up at Chamberlain through helpless eyes.

'You don't understand, my friend. You don't understand.' He passed out.

Chamberlain worked swiftly now, making the tourniquet with pieces of Kaplan's torn clothing and the handle of an umbrella which had hung from the luggage rack.

When at last he had the wound under control, he became conscious of a repeated chanting in the corridor. The words became all too distinct.

'We want food!' The power of a mob formed a jagged image in his mind.

*

In one of the newly attached freight cars two security guards were unpiling the boxes of food from stacks that seemed more than abundant. Each of the cartons was marked: FREEDOM FROM HUNGER/FOOD FROM THE UNITED NATIONS.

'We better move this stuff,' said a guard. 'The natives are getting restless.'

One of the boxes fell to the floor, the top springing open. He stared into the parcel, his eyes dilating. He removed a pocketknife from his trousers and slit the side of another box in one of the piles. A white powder began to leak from it. The other guard was stunned. He let the powder run through his fingers.

The guard with the knife began to jab it through the cardboard of several boxes in different stacks. The white powder trickled from all of them.

'Flour,' he said. 'Bloody flour!'

'Somebody better find an oven,' said the other.

18 11.00 am

Jennifer had been with Yassan for nearly half an hour, though she had only come in passing to moisten his brow. But he had begun to speak, babbling in a delirium, yet revealing to her much that she felt Chamberlain and herself might need in compiling a record of what was happening on that train.

Most of what he had said, however, had lacked coherence, though the threads of authenticity showed through.

'My father is sick,' he murmured now. 'Tell him I have a job ... Promise.'

Jennifer could hear the thunder of the mob from somewhere outside.

'I promise. But you must—'

Relieved, Yassan smiled, not waiting for her to finish.

'My name ... is Yassan. I—'

His mouth opened to form a word, but he lost consciousness.

Jennifer sat by his side, motionless. The door opened and Chamberlain entered breathlessly. He had been searching everywhere for her, and finding her so close to Yassan, he was about to pull her away, when the mob sound grew especially fierce.

'They want food,' Jennifer said. 'Why don't they feed them?'

'It's a lot uglier than that now,' Chamberlain said, reopening the door so that the shouting could be heard more clearly.

'We want food!' the rhythmic chanting bellowed. 'Throw off the Arab! . . . We want food! Throw off the Arab!'

Suddenly one voice rose above the others.

'Kill him!'

This exhortation was followed by a savage cheer.

Chamberlain and Jennifer went into the corridor. Ginger and Parsons were there trying to determine what was happening. Although the growing menace was in the next car, it was plainly coming nearer.

'Need help, pal?' Parsons asked Chamberlain, stopping him by the arm. 'I can use the exercise.'

'Jim will stop them,' Ginger said proudly. 'He's a regular Bogart. . . . Aren't you, darling?'

Parsons shrugged modestly. All four departed in the direction of the chanting, Ginger rolling up her sleeves.

In the next car chaos reigned, as three or four security guards tried unsuccessfully to restore order. There were pushing and shoving of the most violent kind, and the possibility of tragedy at any moment hung in the air like the threat of an electric storm. The guards were pointing their sub-machine guns threateningly, shouting at the passengers to get back, but without effect.

Chamberlain, Jennifer, Parsons and Ginger mingled in the crowd, attempting to help the security guards, but they were thrown about like debris on a heaving sea. Jennifer managed to take some photographs. Parsons, keeping the crowd from crushing them, showed himself as a man of astonishing strength. Chamberlain, seeing the futility of their efforts, however, climbed to a position above the mob and shouted at them.

'Listen!' he cried hoarsely. 'Listen to me!'

They paid him no heed and continued to chant. Then one of the passengers, Gunther, challenged him.

'We've listened enough! We want food!'

The chanting grew louder, the cadence thunderous.

'Your lives are in danger!' Chamberlain shouted.

'Until we get rid of the Arab!' Gunther responded, articulating the mood of the mob, which seemed to certify his leadership. 'Let's get him!' Gunther cried venomously.

The trigger had been pulled. The mob roared like a herd of beasts and surged forward.

Chamberlain threw himself against the tide. He struggled fiercely, every muscle in his body resisting. Parsons, Jennifer, and even Ginger tried to stop them, too. The guards warned that they would open fire, but the mob had gone amok. They broke through, led by Gunther.

Now only Chamberlain stood between them and Yassan. They hurtled towards him like falling boulders. He fought but was swept away in an onslaught of violent blows as the overwhelming human mass beat him to a pulp and he wore blood instead of clothes.

The mob, with Gunther at the head, entered the wagon-lit car, tearing open door after door in search of Yassan. And at last they found him. He lay still as Gunther and some of the others rushed him.

Gunther, his eyes bathed in bile, dragged Yassan up from

the bed with every intention of hurling him into the jaws of the mob. But he looked into Yassan's eyes. They were riveted. Yassan was dead.

Gunther dropped him in horror and everyone drew back, speechless. Chamberlain, who could scarcely remain on his feet, pushed Gunther and the others aside and went to Yassan. He closed his eyelids, then went out into the corridor to stand face to face with the mob. They were silent, limp, spent.

'Now you will listen to me!' Chamberlain cried. They listened. 'The deadliest thing you can do is crowd together. The disease spreads from the man or woman standing next to you.'

This had its calculated effect. Each person seemed to draw away sharply from the next, regarding his neighbour with fear and suspicion.

'Stay apart!' Chamberlain shouted, aware of the divisive effect he was having. 'Every inch increases your chances a thousand times...'

Some passengers returned to their places on the train without hesitation. The guards began to scatter the diehards. The back of the beast had been broken and it fell apart accordingly.

'Break up this death trap!' Chamberlain exhorted finally, staring at Gunther, whose eyes fell.

He turned away and the crowd thinned out rapidly.

Jennifer, Parsons, and Ginger, her hair undone, her blouse torn, came up to Chamberlain. Jennifer dabbed his wounds.

'You were great, doc,' Parsons intoned, shaking Chamberlain's hand.

'Ah!' Ginger sighed magniloquently, 'if I'd had leading men like you!'

They smiled, but their triumph was aborted by Tom. He approached them carrying Susan in his arms. She was unconscious.

'Where do I put her, man?' Tom asked grimly. 'She's got the bug.'

Chamberlain looked at Susan, who showed all the familiar signs. He touched her brow. His face seemed made of tempered steel.

*

The train, following the course of the Danube, was reaching for the Czech border. It streamed ahead like the river itself, its whistle shrieking at the meridian sun.

Saturday

noon to sunset

Kaplan, heavily bandaged, lay on a bed in the empty wagon-lit compartment into which he had been moved. His eyes were closed. He had been given a sedative. Chamberlain stood over him, listening to his chest with a stethoscope. Jennifer was with him.

'He'll be all right,' Chamberlain said. 'Quite an operator. Played sick and scared everyone from the compartment, then he tried to go out with a makeshift battering ram.'

'If we don't hear from Mackenzie soon,' Jennifer replied acidly, 'we might have to try to go out the same way.'

Chamberlain was inscrutable. 'You're the expert,' he said. 'When do we cross?'

'I'd say, in about five, five and a half hours.'

They looked at their watches. There was a soft knock at the door. Chamberlain opened it. A guard motioned to him to follow. They went out.

Kaplan's eyes opened wide. He had heard everything.

Chamberlain accompanied the guard to the priest's compartment in first class. The priest had been watching for them from behind the curtains, and when they arrived he slid the door open slightly and raised the barrel of his gun to the level of their eyes.

'You've got to give me the medicine,' the priest said to Chamberlain.

'The only medicine, "Father", is surrender.'

'Don't shit me, mister!' he shouted jabbing the gun forward. 'It's for the kid . . . She's a little sick.'

A chill ran through Chamberlain's body. 'All right,' he said soothingly. 'But how do I know the child isn't already dead? The disease works *very* quickly, in a matter of hours.'

He was trying to unnerve the priest, to make him think he might lose his hostage. Perhaps there would be a way to rescue the child; perhaps there would be a way to get the gun. There could be no getting off without one.

The priest rolled the door open wide. Catherine, shivering, sweating, torpid, could barely maintain a sitting position. Her hands went up over her eyes to protect them from the light.

'She's got a little fever,' the priest barked with shallow bluster. 'That's all.'

Catherine fell over and lay prostrate across the seats.

'Sit up!' the priest cried, propping her like a puppet. 'You're going to be all right!'

'I'll bring the medicine,' Chamberlain said.

The priest closed the door again leaving space only for the gun to protrude.

'Fast!' he shouted from inside.

*

The Transcontinental Express had entered Czechoslovakia through the Bohemian Forest, crossing the highlands of granite and trees and little else, on a north-easterly route to the Ostrava Crescent. The Milestone computers' optimum course was hardly the shortest in mileage, since any proximity threat to large urban centres, notably Prague, Hradec, Králové, Karvina and Ostrava, had to be scrupulously avoided. Nevertheless, by sifting data from the UIC memory tapes furnished by Paris, the computers had coordinated a low-trafficked route, however circuitous, which was calculated to consume less time than any other, even the most direct. This had required complete right-of-way and the cancellation of several hundred scheduled domestic and some international trips by other trains, which wreaked havoc on local travel plans and arrangements, though no one would ever know why.

The train had crossed Bohemia and Moravia in record time, and at the moment was winding into the Alp-like Carpathians, where its route would be particularly roundabout. Before long, however, it would pass a tourist sign written in four languages: Czech, Slovak, German and English, which would read: 'Jablunkov Pass, High Tatra Range, Carpathian Mountains, Altitude 7,112 feet'.

*

At the Milestone Command Centre, Mackenzie was turning the pages of a copy of *National Geographic*. His eyes fell on a striking photograph of the Jablunkov Pass, part of a series to illustrate the text of an article entitled, 'The Cassandra Crossing'. Another photograph showed a huge, wooden, bridge-like structure linking the towering peaks of two mountains. The caption read: 'The eighteenth-century Cassandra Crossing – *which straw will break the camel's back?*'

Hoffmann spoke, looking over Mackenzie's shoulder. 'The article is based on interviews with shepherds, hearsay, local folklore. Hardly scientific.' He could not have been more disdainful.

Mackenzie looked up at Elena, then at the programmer.

'The crossing is weak, true,' the programmer reported to him. 'But it can take a much heavier load than our train. We ran a check against official data.'

'*What* official data?' Mackenzie demanded sharply.

'A full-scale engineering survey done after the article came out,' Elena replied. 'And a spot check made less than two hours ago. Prague sent in a helicopter full of experts.'

The programmer pointed to the photograph of the crossing. 'Straw on the camel's back, my ass! We're a fly on the Brooklyn Bridge!'

Mackenzie glared disapprovingly. Elena knew this was not the kind of information he sought.

'The computer says,' she told him calmly, 'the risk is zero, zero, zero.'

Mackenzie nodded thoughtfully. He picked up the telephone.

'Get me Chamberlain,' he said.

*

Called to the radio-telephone, Chamberlain, and Jennifer on an auxiliary receiver, listened to the report from Milestone.

'Let me put it bluntly, Mackenzie,' Chamberlain said in reply. 'How do we know you're telling us the truth?'

'Do you take me for a mass murderer?' Mackenzie shot back angrily. He checked himself, breathed deeply, and tried to reason with him. 'Listen, Chamberlain, I'm in a situation where I have to trade one risk for another. Even if there were a slight chance of Miss Saint being right – and I'm convinced there is none – I would still send the train on ahead...'

He paused and looked at Elena, who felt the full weight of the decision he had made. Then he continued with inescapable logic.

'You have hundreds of sick people on board by now, a limited supply of oxygen, and no place else to go that isn't days farther from where you are now. I'd be trading off a slight chance for no chance at all that you'd survive.' He paused again, then reached out to him. 'You are my witness, Chamberlain. I have done all that I can.'

Chamberlain and Jennifer could not help but be impressed by Mackenzie's sincerity. Chamberlain replied sympathetically but firmly.

'What we have all done: elevate science above more ancient wisdom ... then place our bets on technology and machines, and hope for the best. That's not enough, Mackenzie.' He added what was almost a threat. 'And a few of us don't like the odds.'

Mackenzie grimaced. He looked up at the large tape machine marked 'Top Secret: for Milestone Reference Only', then at its switch engraved, 'Destruct'. He replied with finality.

'We meet in Poland, Dr Chamberlain.'

He hung up.

'I'll bet he's a damn good surgeon!' he exclaimed.

'You two are really so much alike,' Elena remarked. Her eyes were kind.

Mackenzie grew museful. 'There's a difference,' he said. 'Chamberlain is concerned with people. And I ... with numbers.'

20 2.00 pm

In the communications car, Chamberlain looked at Jennifer almost apologetically, but there was a light in Jennifer's eyes.

'Did you hear what he said?' she asked excitedly.

He was somewhat puzzled. 'It all comes back to Cassandra.'

She brushed his words aside. 'Not that! ... He said by now we have hundreds of sick people on board!'

Chamberlain's brow knitted as he began to perceive what she was driving at.

'We sure were supposed to,' she went on. 'What did they say? Twelve hours? Well, we've been on this miserable train for over twenty-six ... and how many do we have? Three humans, one dog!'

Chamberlain formulated no reply. He shouted at the radio operator.

'Get Mackenzie back!'

The operator tried to reconnect them, but everything froze when the door slid open with a crash. Two unarmed guards entered backing in at the prodding of a gun – in the hands of the priest, who dragged Catherine with him.

'This time I'll tell them myself!' the priest blared frenziedly. 'We're getting off now, not later!'

His hand tightened around Catherine's arm. She cried out weakly in pain, kicking him.

'You're hurting her!' Chamberlain roared.

'Call!' the priest ordered the operator, paying no attention to Chamberlain.

Chamberlain suddenly stared at the priest with a pretended air of concern. He saw this and it made him feel uneasy.

'The medicine is your only chance,' Chamberlain said to him pacifyingly. '*You've* got it now.'

He reached into his pocket for his stethoscope and approached him.

'Don't move!' the priest warned.

'Look at you,' Chamberlain said still moving towards him cautiously. 'You're sweating, you're fidgety ... anxious. All the classic symptoms.'

Playing on his panic, Chamberlain raised the stethoscope to the priest's chest. He recoiled at first, but, holding the gun on Catherine, he allowed him to listen.

Chamberlain shook his head ruefully. He removed the stethoscope from his ears and handed it to the priest.

'Listen yourself.'

The priest stared terrifiedly. Chamberlain brought the listening ends of the stethoscope towards the priest's ears. The gun was touching Catherine's temple. She stood motionless, as did everyone else in the room. The priest put up his free hand to take the chest-piece of the stethoscope.

With a lightning move, Chamberlain twisted the rubber tubes of the instrument around the priest's neck, forcing the chest-piece against his throat. Chamberlain drew it as tight as a noose and wound himself around him. The priest's hands shot up to his neck to struggle against the instrument which was rapidly strangling him, and his gun was momentarily pointed in a harmless direction.

Jennifer seized Catherine.

Now everyone could only look on in horror as Chamberlain and the priest were locked in a life or death embrace.

Chamberlain gripped the priest's wrist trying to keep the gun pointed away from himself and squeeze it from his hand. The gun went off. A bullet ripped through the radio-telephone making brilliant sparks in the oxygen-charged atmosphere. The radio burst into flames. The operator reached for a fire extinguisher and battled with the raging blaze.

Chamberlain and the priest fought on, each one tearing at the other in a savage test of strength. The pendulum sprung back and forth. Only by the sheer power of his surgeon's hands did Chamberlain manage to stay alive.

The fire roared with white flames. Chamberlain and the priest lay on the floor struggling with each other and to keep away from the fire. Jennifer shielded Catherine, her eyes pinned to Chamberlain.

A shot rang out. The two men broke apart. The gun scrambled across the floor. The priest rose quickly to his feet and ran wildly towards the next car. Chamberlain went after him. Jennifer followed. Catherine drew back into a far corner, the flames flickering in her eyes.

The priest ran desperately in the direction opposite the engine, Chamberlain in pursuit. Passengers were bowled over. A guard shouted at him to stop. He shoved him aside violently. Another guard raised his handgun, took aim, and killed the priest without hesitation.

The passengers screamed. Chamberlain and Jennifer stared in horror at the guard who had felled the unarmed, bogus priest.

They rushed back to the communications car, where the fire continued to rage. They joined the others in fighting the flames with extinguishers. After a while, the fire was brought under control.

The guards dragged the priest's body into the car. The medical personnel had brought a steel coffin. While they busied themselves in restoring order, Jennifer comforted Catherine. Chamberlain, seeing the priest's gun lying unnoticed under a table, moved stealthily towards it, seized it, and slipped it into his pocket.

He returned to Jennifer's side. In awful silence, they looked together at the most serious damage done by the fire. The radio-telephone had been totally destroyed, consumed. There could be no further communication with Milestone.

21 3.10pm

The Cassandra Crossing was built between 1760 and 1762 by Johannes and Hans Ulrich Grubenmann, two Swiss carpenters, who in the previous five years had completed two timber bridges over the Rhine at Schauffhausen and a similar but larger one at Reichenau.

The wooden construction in the High Tatras bridged a gap of 932 feet and stood 211 feet above the void it traversed. It had been ordered by the then ruling Hapsburg, Francis I of Lorraine, to be exact – Holy Roman Emperor and husband of Maria Theresa, Queen of Hungary and Bohemia. Francis had been in one of those perennially recurring royal moods of wanting to consolidate his kingdoms and his military advisers had proffered the age-old suggestion of bridge-building.

The crossing, since there was no water below – except during the spring thaw when the melting slopes formed a shallow but fast-running stream which invariably ran dry by mid-June – was essentially a trestle. Far more easy for the Grubenmanns to build than the Rhine bridges, it consisted of a horizontal ground sill, slightly inclined legs sunk into the bedrock, and a horizontal top transom, all of which were stiffened by diagonal braces, erector-set style.

When completed, Francis sent the bishop of Ostrava to bless it, and the prelate named it after the carpenters, calling it 'Prejezd Grubenmann'. For a while it was considered a local marvel, but it was rarely used, and, at least by Francis and his heirs, totally forgotten.

It was not until the coming of the railway age, a full century and a quarter later, that the Grubenmann Crossing came once again to the attention of the distant authorities (still the Hapsburgs, still for military purposes), at which time tracks were laid, traffic increased considerably, and the foundations, however briefly waterlogged once each year, began to sink appreciably.

In the driest season of 1892, a shepherd wandering below the structure carved a notch in one of the legs to mark what seemed to him the amount the supports had fallen: about half an inch. He reported this to a friend in his village who was reputed to be acquainted with someone who knew the provincial mayor, predicting that the crossing would shortly collapse.

An investigation was undertaken, and while there could be no doubt that the Grubenmann opus stood a half-inch less tall than when new, this was considered far better than normal, a testament to the master craftsmanship of old. The shepherd, through the same channels he had employed, was told not to worry, to stop spreading fear, and by implication, that he would otherwise be taken as daft.

The following year, the shepherd, who had spent much of the cold months thinking and asking his peers and his elders about the nature of wood, discovered another half-inch descent. He made a second notch and some new grim predictions, which brought only scorn to his name, at least from the local officialdom. The process continued, including the slow descent of the trestle, and before very long some people said he was silly, others a seeker after attention, and, it seems, no less than one person called him a 'Kasandruv'.

The shepherd died in anonymity some years later, apparently long before his time, and without doubt in some measure of humiliation. But he did live to carve ten notches measuring four inches and to witness both a general reinforcement of the crossing in 1900 and, in spite of that, its sinking continue. He was no longer around, however, when some of his younger neighbours took to adding notches each year, forecasting calamity soon, and calling the *prejezd* itself '*Kasandruv*'. In the way these things often happen, the Grubenmanns fell into obscurity, the shepherd gained posthumous local credence and honour, and the *prejezd* became known far and wide as the Cassandra Crossing.

*

On the day the Transcontinental Express was swallowing all the iron not two whole hours west of Cassandra, the crossing seemed a deserted tangle of wizened wood rising fragilely to the azure sky of a brilliant afternoon. It stood between the silent peaks like something lame on crutches, capable of being swept away by an angry wind, yet at the same time not without the nobility of an old master and the majesty of having seen two hundred years. But the weeds of neglect grew in the cross-ties and the last notch in the leg, cut a mere fortnight ago, lay higher than the first by more than two feet.

*

On the train, Chamberlain was examining the baby, who no longer appeared feverish, nor was he crying. Indeed, he gurgled and smiled under Chamberlain's touch.

'He doesn't look too bad, does he?' Chamberlain said to Jennifer, who took the playful infant into her arms.

'No one is sick on this train! No one!' she said, cradling the baby. 'It's some kind of cruel mistake.'

Chamberlain shook his head negatively, thinking aloud.

'Yassan ... a positive diagnosis from the dog.... No, it's more complex.'

They went out. Chamberlain wanted to check on Catherine. They walked to her new compartment in silence, Chamberlain reaching for an explanation.

'I'm a man who works with his hands, not with theories,' he said, after finding Catherine resting comfortably, apparently recovering rapidly. 'But I know that in the evolution of disease bacteria there were countless deadly strains *too* specialized for their environment. *Too* fit for survival.'

'Like the dinosaurs,' Jennifer suggested, 'dying off when their environment changed.'

They went to check on Susan.

'No,' Chamberlain replied, 'probably more like man. Killing off his environment ... destroying his means of survival.'

Susan sat in bed, smiling her pretty smile, her old Long Island hedonistic self again. Chamberlain listened with his stethoscope to her very healthy looking chest.

'This train had a perfect environment for the growth of disease,' he said to Jennifer, while Susan studied him dreamily. 'But only four living things got sick ... and all had physical contact with Yassan. The germs couldn't spread easily.'

'They were so damn content with Yassan's body,' Jennifer said, understanding Chamberlain's reasoning. 'Fat cats!'

Chamberlain finished his examination and smiled optimistically at Susan. There was an amorous glow in her eyes.

'I wonder how you look in your uniform,' she said, drawing a puzzled expression from Chamberlain and Jennifer, but lingering all the while in her fantasy.

In the corridor, Chamberlain summed up his theory.

'A unique environment created a unique race of bacteria. Feeble. Doomed from the start. The few who managed to strike were no match for the body's natural defences.'

'Whatever it was,' Jennifer responded pragmatically, 'there's not much point left in testing the Cassandra Crossing, is there?'

Chamberlain peered into her eyes, then turned to look out the window. The train was taking a curve around a mountain. There was not much he could see, except the tail and the engine, but he knew what lay not far enough beyond.

Suddenly, as if by common tacit consent, they were hurrying to the front of the train. They were stopped by two guards protecting the access to the locomotive and they argued with them desperately, seeking permission to speak to the officer in command.

Some passengers, drawn by the disturbance, entered the corridor and watched with curiosity.

Finally, the guards permitted Chamberlain to pass, but not Jennifer. He went into the next car. Jennifer retreated reluctantly, and when she noticed some of the passengers looking at her strangely, she wheeled to them.

'We have to stop the train!' she cried.

To them she appeared mad. She turned around. The others regarded her similarly. Her eyes narrowed. She could feel the curse of Cassandra possessing her.

Chamberlain had got as far as the door to the engineer's cab, when the guards intervened again. He tried to explain and, failing to make the slightest impression, he struggled with them.

'There's no reason to go on!' he shouted trying to force his way through. The guards held him back. The door to the cab opened and the fireman looked out to see what the commotion was all about. Chamberlain seized the chance and threw himself inside.

The guards began to drag him out. The engineer was aghast as Chamberlain threw hand and fist at the mysterious handles and switches of his controls. The guards hauled him back. He saw an electronic coupling device glowing green and he plunged forward to get at it. A guard inside tackled him, throwing him to the floor. Another put his handgun to Chamberlain's head. He stared into the slit-eyes of the masked man, and thought of the priest. The eyes, it seemed to him, were those of the man who had slain him. The guard cocked his gun. He wore the captain's bars. Chamberlain backed off, futility forged cold in his face.

22 3.50pm

Ginger was seated at a table with a linen napkin on her lap, a knife, a fork, a glass of water, and a plate filled with a heaping portion of flour. With the knife in her right hand, she cut it into two separate piles, put down the knife, and, American style, switched her fork to her right and began to eat.

Parsons, who had not been paying any attention to her, suddenly saw her eating and looked at her incredulously.

'Not very tasty,' she said taking a forkful, 'but it contains most of the ingredients of cake and biscuits, quiche lorraine, croissants and pizza. Of course, you have to add water.' She took the merest sip from her glass and frowned as if it contained vinegar. '*That* has got to go!'

She got up, collared a fresh bottle of whisky from her suitcase, and slugged hard.

'Ah!' she sighed. 'They can keep their wheat ... as long as I have my rye!'

Chamberlain entered with Jennifer. Ginger tried unsuccessfully to hide the bottle, and thinking she had managed to do so, she turned to her plate of flour as if she had been eating it all along.

'Welcome,' she said gaily. 'We were having our free lunch. Just like an airline.'

Chamberlain, making certain the door had been closed behind him, spoke directly to Parsons.

'The train has to be stopped.'

Parsons' face gnarled. Jennifer picked up the thread.

'I've been through this country. We're approaching a military base with a powerful radio transmitter,' she said. 'That means some of us will have to get off.'

All this could have but scarce significance for Parsons, uninformed as he was, and they knew it. Chamberlain appealed to him on a more basic level.

'We could use a good man, Parsons.'

Parsons threw a distasteful glance at the flour and water, but seemed noncommittal.

'*I'll* go, darling,' Ginger intoned. 'I adore adventure.'

'There's a high risk, Ginger,' Chamberlain replied with restrained scepticism. 'It will be an ordeal.'

Ginger brushed the thought away. 'Hardship means nothing to me,' she said. 'I crossed an entire desert working for de Mille.... In a Cadillac, of course, but those were the days before air conditioning.'

Chamberlain could only remain politely dubious, but at last Parsons replied.

'Where's out, pal?'

Chamberlain withdrew the priest's gun. He set it in the firing position. Parsons was thoughtful for a moment. He seemed on the verge of making a decision of great personal meaning. He looked at Ginger, then at Chamberlain.

'I haven't done much with my life, doc,' he began, 'but I guess stopping an armoured train on its way to Poland is no small thing.' He shrugged. 'I'll go.'

Ginger stroked his hair tenderly. There was an exchange of smiles, but suddenly the door swung open. Kaplan, looking as good as new, stepped inside wearing his widest grin.

'I'll go, too!' he exclaimed.

Parsons was infuriated by the intrusion.

'Who the fuck are you?' he demanded.

'I'm the ghost of a thousand deaths,' Kaplan all but sang. 'I've got eleven languages on my tongue, including Polish,

Czech and Slovak. And I can run very fast ... You said you could use a good man.'

They all looked at one another. There was common assent. Chamberlain nodded to Kaplan, who seemed immensely relieved. Chamberlain glanced at his watch, then to Jennifer.

'I think you should all know why this action is necessary,' he said to the others.

*

Mackenzie was with Elena at the wall screen. The image projected was the map giving the train's position.

'The only contact we have left is the remote sensing device,' Mackenzie informed her.

They looked at the map. The flashing red light showed the train to be closing in on the Cassandra Crossing, which was indicated by a series of hairlines across the train's route and a hand-lettered place name of recent insertion, marked 'Cassandra'. The distance on the map was less than an inch, by the scale some thirty miles. The computer projected an estimated time of arrival of sixty-seven point eight minutes, or precisely 5.13 p.m.

'What if you had to stop the train?' Elena asked.

'We could do that at any point through the regular railway signalling system.' He searched her face. 'Why?' he asked provocatively. 'You're not being seduced by Cassandra?'

Elena did not answer. A telephone rang. Mackenzie picked it up and listened with annoyance.

'Dog? What dog?'

With an expression of surprise he turned back to the wall screen. A televised image of Oscar was flashed. In sharp contrast with his previous appearance, the dog was lively now, playing boisterously with the team of scientists who had attended him, and clearly fully recovered.

Mackenzie slowly returned the phone to its cradle. He was lost in thought.

*

At the end of a corridor in the second-class car adjoining the wagon-lits, Chamberlain appeared behind one of the guards, pressed his gun into the man's ribs, and disarmed him.

At the other end of the same corridor, Parsons over-powered a guard with his bare hands, relieving him of his weapons.

Kaplan came by and bound the guard's hands and feet with belts taken from suitcases. He did the same to the man Chamberlain held at bay. The three of them repeated the process once more and within minutes four guards had been neutralized, none of the others the wiser.

Jennifer, in her compartment, was hurriedly packing her camera equipment. Her door was open. She saw Kaplan and Parsons rush by. They carried sub-machine guns. Jennifer stepped into the corridor. Passengers were milling about confusedly.

'What's happening?' some shouted when they saw her. 'What's going on?' The corridor filled up quickly.

Jennifer said nothing, edging her way forward. Her eyes sought out Chamberlain. At last he entered coming from the second-class car. He smiled triumphantly and pushed to-wards her to join her. The passengers stared at him expec-tantly. He spoke to them sombrely.

'We have taken over two cars.'

*

Mackenzie had summoned Hoffmann and Elena with an air of crisis that puzzled them.

'How many passengers should already have the disease?' Mackenzie demanded of Hoffmann.

'More than half – about seven hundred – conservatively speaking, of course.'

Elena's eyes widened. Mackenzie turned to her.

'How many had Chamberlain reported?'

'Three.'

Hoffmann registered extreme surprise. Mackenzie snapped his eyes back to him.

'Hoffmann, I assume you have kept a living culture of the micro-organism taken from the dog.'

'Of course. That is standard pro—'

'I want you to place it in an environment as close as possible to the one we created on the train. I want to know what effect that has on its communicability. I want to know this in minutes not hours!'

'You can't be serious!' Hoffmann was shocked. 'There are too many unknowns. At best we can only get an approximation, and even that would take—'

'Minutes, Hoffmann, minutes!' He looked up at the clock. 'You have sixty-three of them!'

'This is totally unorthodox!' Hoffmann protested. 'We are scientists! We have a method!'

Mackenzie simply stared at him with glacial determination. Elena breathed with immense relief, as if everything would come up right in the end.

'Very well!' Hoffmann said at last. 'The responsibility is yours!'

Mackenzie felt every crushing ounce of his responsibility.

23 4.25 pm

Kaplan was holding a sub-machine gun on one of the captured guards – though not very attentively since he was paying more mind to what Chamberlain was saying to a group of assembled passengers.

'I've explained the risk in going on ahead,' Chamberlain was saying. 'The risk in getting off is probably much greater.'

He glanced at Jennifer. She accepted this. 'But any of you,' he went on, 'is welcome to come if you wish.'

The guard in Kaplan's neglected charge was bound at his feet and his wrists, but he was rapidly succeeding in freeing himself.

'We're nearing a climb up a mountain,' Chamberlain told the bewildered passengers. 'The train will have to reduce speed ... I can give you only two minutes to decide.' He looked at his watch.

A familiar voice shouted from the crowd.

'You'll get us all killed!'

Chamberlain looked around. It was Steward Tickler, floridly defiant.

'Why should anyone listen to you, Chamberlain?' he raged hysterically. 'You've pirated this train. You've told us lies! Leave us alone!'

Chamberlain was compassionate. 'You *are* alone. Very much alone.' He turned to the others. 'Who's coming? This is your only chance.'

The steward drew back into a corner, as the passengers looked to one another wondering who, if anyone, would be the first.

A soldier took a step forward as if to go, but he was stopped by his comrade, who with a penetrating look of fear convinced him to stay behind.

No one moved. Gunther waved his hand in a gesture of scepticism. The mother of the baby who had recovered clutched the infant to her breast. A man studied his frightened wife and children, then shook his head no.

By now, the guard had completely unbound himself. He pretended otherwise.

Parsons, standing watch at the end of the corridor which gave on to the cars beyond the two captured, looked through the doorway window across the connecting bridge. He could see the guard in the next car, who was unaware of the escape now in progress. The guard seemed to catch his gaze and peered back suspiciously. Parsons drew up against the wall. The guard watched for a moment or two, then turned away.

The American students were speaking among themselves.

'I'm going, man,' Tom announced.

'Don't be an idiot!' Betty whispered harshly. 'When we get to the camp, they'll send us back in style, or we sue! ... I mean, *and* we sue!'

'*If* you get to the camp,' Tom rejoined, smiling.

'You don't believe that crap about the crossing, do you?'

'Well,' Tom reasoned, 'I figure it this way: Cassandra was ripped off by Apollo because she wouldn't ball him. So he laid this curse on her. That's where his head was at, not mine.' He started to go, then looked back. 'He was pissed, but he never made her a liar.'

He edged through the crowd towards the front, all eyes on him. Steward Tickler suddenly grabbed Tom's sleeve in an attempt to stop him. Tom shoved him aside brusquely.

Little Catherine, pale, somewhat unsteady on her legs, was wandering about confusedly among the passengers. She came up to Ginger and tugged on her blouse.

'Am I all better now?' she asked.

Ginger put her hands to Catherine's cheeks affectionately. 'Of course, love. But go back to your compartment now ... and Auntie Ginger will take care of you.'

Catherine turned, trying to remember exactly where her compartment was. Finally, she nodded decisively and strayed away. She passed the guard who had secretly freed himself and saw him inching forward on the floor. She wondered what it was all about.

Ginger went up to Jennifer, forcing a smile. She removed a tawdrily jewelled ring from her finger and closed it in Jennifer's hand.

'Nothing personal, love,' she whispered. 'I believe you and all that. But somebody's got to entertain the camp ... and it's not going to be Bob Hope.'

Jennifer was disappointed but understanding. 'But you have to come, Ginger. Jim ... we all need you.'

'Thank you, darling. But last year's chickens are not as tough as they taste.' She was on the verge of tears, but smiling still. 'As Sam Goldwyn once told me, "Include me out" ...'

Jennifer squeezed Ginger's hand, realizing that any further appeal would be useless if not cruel.

'By the way,' Ginger almost sobbed, 'tell Jim I love him. Tell him ... he's a champion.'

They embraced.

Parsons had further aroused the suspicions of the guard in the next car, who now stared hard and long across the connecting bridge. The guard began to approach with caution. Parsons lay in wait. The guard entered. Parsons attacked without hesitation, driving the muzzle of his gun against the guard's head.

'You've had it, pal!' he whispered hoarsely.

The guard ceded. Parsons looked back into the next car. Two other guards were at the far end, approaching suspiciously.

The time was up for the passengers and Chamberlain looked around to see if anyone had accepted his offer. There were no takers, except for Tom, who pushed forward, exchanging friendly nods with Chamberlain.

It was time to go. Kaplan began to approach them, too, but the guard who had freed himself suddenly pounced on him and seized his sub-machine gun. Kaplan fell to the floor. The guard pointed the weapon at Chamberlain.

All the passengers drew back in fear.

The guard motioned to Chamberlain, who stood near the exit door, to drop his gun. Chamberlain obeyed.

Tom, now at the head of the passenger group, came up quietly behind the guard, removing from safe keeping the book of matches he had concealed. He stole close to the guard, struck a match, and touched the white flame to the gauze of the guard's protective clothing.

Instantly, he burst into a tower of screaming fire, a human torch. In his last agonizing moments, he fired the sub-machine gun wildly, and his weapon dropped from his fiery hands.

The passengers recoiled, but the bullets had found a mark – nailing the baby's mother to the wall. Her eyes sprung open in the shape of two zeros as she slid slowly to the floor in death. The baby crept away unharmed. Susan picked him up, holding him tightly, as if he were her own.

'Get him off!' Tom shouted to Chamberlain.

Chamberlain picked up the guard's gun and shot open the door. It swung wide, the forward movement of the train driving it back against the side of the car. A gale of de-compression whirled inside, as Tom charged behind the flam-ing, shrieking guard and shoved him off the train. A ball of fire rolled down the mountainside.

Everyone was momentarily still. Parsons, holding his sub-machine gun on the guard he had overpowered, backed through the passengers towards Chamberlain.

'C'mon, doc! I'm cooling off!' he shouted.

Chamberlain glanced outside the open door. The train was climbing, its speed diminishing, but hardly a crawl. The un-even ground beneath him rushed by.

The guards in the adjoining car, hearing the disturbance, ran to the connecting bridge to the escape corridor. Parsons had wedged the door, but he knew it could not hold for very long.

Chamberlain nodded to Jennifer. She leaned out for the jump, her camera slung around her. She was ready. Their eyes met.

'Good luck, Jennifer Saint,' he said strangely. 'I've got to try from inside.'

Jennifer was stunned. She was about to reply, but the guards from the other car had forced their way.

'Jump!' Parsons cried.

One of the guards fired. Chamberlain was hit. His gun fell and he slumped to the floor holding his leg. Jennifer froze.

The guards rushed to the door. Kaplan stared in utter horror. He took a deep breath, and cried out from the very pit of his soul.

'I've got to get off!'

He charged the guard at the door, throwing him from the train. Then, he jumped.

Another guard leaned out and fired.

Kaplan rolled over on the ground, sprung to his feet and ran. Another shot rang out. Kaplan was hit. His hands went up. He dropped.

The train climbed away. A guard jumped. He carried a flamethrower.

Kaplan lay flat on the ground. Even now he could not resist Talmudic commentary.

'Now you see it,' he muttered faintly. 'Now you don't.... Now...'

Kaplan was dead. His hands crossed his chest: a different watch on each wrist.

The guard with the flamethrower stood spreadeagled over him. He set Kaplan ablaze.

A remaining guard on the train stood over Chamberlain, forcing Jennifer, Parsons and Tom further back in the car. Chamberlain clutched the bullet wound in his leg. Jennifer tried to go to him, but she was thrust backward rudely by the guard, who allowed Ginger, however, to remain at Chamberlain's side.

Chamberlain looked up at Ginger, then at the guard. He was closing the exit door. Chamberlain winced in pain.

On the Milestone wall screen the flashing red light showed Cassandra to lie within seventeen miles of the Transcontinental Express. The train was averaging fifty miles an hour, giving an estimated time of arrival of twenty point four minutes.

At the crossing itself, a shepherd named Jan Cieszyn was moving his flock alongside the tracks. He could look across the western mountain folds to hills of green, and in the very distance, almost smaller than an eye could perceive, he saw the train, moving as slowly as the hour-hand of a clock but with the same relentless inevitability. He was startled. No train of such dimensions had ever passed this way.

Mackenzie watched the map on the wall screen with one hand on the telephone, awaiting word from Dr Hoffmann. Everyone else in the room stared at the red light in equal suspense of the outcome.

'If you have any doubts,' Elena whispered to him, 'why don't you stop the train?'

'And do what?' he flared. 'As of now, Elena, we've proved only one thing: The greatest danger to those passengers is time ... time lost in getting to the camp.' He reflected a moment. 'Hoffmann is right. We are scientists. We need proof!' His voice fell to a bitter mumble. 'Men do not stand naked before their gods.'

'Poor men,' Elena said with sadness.

The flock of sheep were grazing on the grass that grew between the tracks.

*

Two guards were working on resealing the abortive escape door. Ginger tried to comfort Chamberlain, offering him a slug from a bottle of rye.

'Never fear, darling,' she said. 'Jim'll save us.'

Chamberlain refused the drink. Ginger took a very long

one herself, and when she looked down, he was gone. One of the guards noticed his disappearance and took after him. Ginger tried to slow him by stepping in his way, but he pushed her aside violently. He took aim at Chamberlain, who was staggering down the corridor.

Ginger smashed her whisky bottle over the guard's head, knocking him unconscious.

'That's what I call a Canadian club!' she exclaimed, surprised at her own capability.

The other guard saw what was happening and shouted a warning. Parsons seized the unconscious guard's gun and shot the second guard dead, quickly stripping him of his weapons and flamethrower and handing the latter to Tom.

'Let's shoot this thing open again, man!' Tom cried to Chamberlain, while tying up the unconscious guard.

'Too late!' Chamberlain called back. 'We're on the downgrade!'

He turned and continued along the corridor. Tom and Parsons caught up with him, handing him a gun. Jennifer and Ginger stood guard.

The train raced in swift descent, gaining speed, losing the brief time that remained to Cassandra. The shepherd saw the train clearly now and began to drive his flock from the tracks.

*

Milestone waited, unmoving, as if trapped in a photograph.

'Madness!' Mackenzie cried to no one in particular. 'A ninety-million-dollar scientific programme worried about a Greek legend ridiculed in Homer's time.'

His jaw was tight, pulsating.

*

Chamberlain, wracked with pain and dripping with sweat, stood with Tom and Parsons at the diaphragm connecting bridge giving on to the next forward car. Passengers stared at them hypnotically, immobile.

'No danger from the rear,' Parsons reported. 'All the guards are gone, tied or dead.'.

'Think we can make it to the engine?' Tom asked.

Chamberlain motioned to them to look ahead. They peered through the double windows on either side of the diaphragm. Three guards were entering the next car, their guns at the ready.

Chamberlain slowly opened the door to the diaphragm. He crossed the bridge and slid the next door slightly ajar. The guards fired. Passengers screamed. Chamberlain returned their fire.

Steward Tickler ran into the corridor, shouting distraughtly.

'Stop it, Chamberlain! Stop—'

A guard fired. His bullet killed the steward.

'Forget the engine!' Chamberlain said to Tom and Parsons. 'It's suicide!'

They dropped to the floor dodging a bullet.

The exchange of gunfire rapidly developed into a stand-off, the guards retreating to the safety of the previous car, leaving a clear corridor between themselves and Chamberlain. But the shooting continued sporadically.

Chamberlain shouted to the terrified passengers in the besieged car.

'There's a crossing up ahead!' he cried out through a sally of crossfire. 'It's going to collapse! We are cutting ourselves loose!'

Tom and Parsons looked at him incredulously. The passengers remained paralysed. Chamberlain, with one of the sub-machine guns, began to riddle the floor of the connecting bridge, cutting away a rectangle of steel above the coupling device which linked the two cars.

One passenger suddenly made a run in an attempt to reach Chamberlain's position. He was killed instantly by the guards, but in the confusion two other passengers got through and Tom and Parsons pulled them to safety.

Chamberlain lifted part of the steel floor he had shot away. The coupler lay beneath them exposed. The ground below and the blur of cross-ties in the roadbed rushed by noisily under the steel knuckles that held the two cars together.

Chamberlain began to fire the flamethrower at the coupling device and bursts of flame soon made the steel glow red.

*

By now, the flashing red light on the wall screen map was virtually superimposed on the Cassandra Crossing, yet a hairline of seven minutes remained. Mackenzie stood close to the map. The red light throbbed cruelly on the mirror of his eyes.

*

Jan Cieszyn was having difficulty removing his flock from the tracks. The sheep seemed disoriented, disturbed, singularly defiant. The beasts he had driven from the tracks were returning.

25 5.08 pm

Like the shepherd, Jennifer and Ginger, in the relative safety of the wagon-lit car, were trying to gather the passengers together for a retreat further to the rear.

Jennifer looked into the compartment where Catherine had been placed for recovery. It was empty.

'Have you seen Catherine?' Jennifer asked Ginger urgently.

'I told her to wait in her compartment.'

Jennifer stared at her with desperation, realization entering her like a knife.

'Oh, my God!' she cried. 'She must have gone back! Her *old* compartment!'

Jennifer turned and ran towards the head of the train.

*

Tom had taken over the task of firing the coupler, while Chamberlain banged on it with the steel butt of his gun. It glowed bright red under the steady stream of flame. Parsons covered them.

Jennifer came tearing through. Parsons stopped her.

'Catherine!' she shouted at Chamberlain. 'She's up ahead!'

She tried to break away from Parsons. Chamberlain grabbed her, hurled her back, and started to go himself.

She clawed at him, trying to stop him.

'You'll be killed!'

Chamberlain threw her back forcefully into Tom's hands, freeing himself.

'Promise you'll call me sometime,' he said. 'I'm in the phone book.'

He entered the forward part of the train. Jennifer was torn. She mouthed the words, 'I promise ... I promise.'

Chamberlain, who could not remember in which compartment Catherine had been, began to search for her one by one, calling out her name frantically.

Parsons took over the task of banging on the coupler.

'You'll never break it that way!' Jennifer said to him. 'It's not possible. There's an electronic device in the engine. The contacts are under the knuckles!'

Parsons looked at her for a moment, then tried to reach below, pulling his hand away painfully. Now, he would have to wait for the coupler to cool.

The minutes had burned away. Only seconds remained. The engineer saw the sheep on the tracks. He began to brake the train. Jan Cieszyn whipped his beasts. At last they responded, fearful of their own lives. They opened the way to the threshold of the Cassandra Crossing.

'Catherine!' Chamberlain thundered.

His only answer was the whine of a bullet whizzing by.

He opened another door. Catherine was inside. She sat in a corner, blowing bubbles through the wire ring. He grabbed her into his arms. Her bubble ring dropped to the floor. She tried to retrieve it. But Chamberlain swept her up and dashed outside.

The engine of the Transcontinental Express was already on the crossing. In braking the train's forward movement, the engineer had not yet increased his velocity waiting to get to the other side. But the train went on, and now two cars, three, four, were on the crossing. It was holding.

*

Mackenzie waited at the telephone with inhuman patience – and inhuman anguish – a man with twelve hundred souls on his back.

*

Parsons had located the cable under the coupler, which led to the pressure points linking the system from car to car. The cable, swathed in steel, was itself still too hot to touch, but he prodded it with his gun, trying to break it away. Sparks flew.

*

Nine cars were on the crossing. It seemed to sag. The train slowed to a crawl. Ten cars. Eleven.

*

Chamberlain, carrying Catherine, was returning, but his path was blocked by disoriented passengers filling the corridor. He forced his way ahead.

Suddenly a loud crack was heard. The train seemed to drop a few inches in the way an elevator settles sinking stomachs. Everyone shrieked. But the crossing held. The train went on. The guards, however, gave up the fight, and began banging their guns against the windows trying to break through.

Parsons was unable to dislocate the cable. His hands were burned, the flesh torn away.

A second crack.

Passengers were leaping across the open floor in the diaphragm, using Parsons' body as a bridge. But the train remained coupled.

Still another crack. Still the train inched forward, like a wriggling worm. Almost all of thirteen cars were on the Cassandra Crossing – 22,900 tons.

Chamberlain neared the end of the thirteenth car. Jennifer pulled passengers to safety shouting him on.

The Cassandra Crossing collapsed. Slowly, brace by brace turning downward as if relieved of the burden of centuries.

The coupler snapped in two like a stick. Jennifer yanked Parsons to her.

The Transcontinental Express began to fall, leaning into the chasm, arching like a frightened cat. Chamberlain was at the broken end of the forward part. He hurled Catherine across a gap of nearly five feet. Jennifer caught her.

'Jump!' she cried to Chamberlain.

Chamberlain leaped. But the distance had widened. He could not bridge it. He fell to the sharply sloping mountainside and disappeared from view.

The train went down. Inside, passengers were smashed against the walls and the ceilings. Gravity seemed to have gone mad, yet it would rule the day.

As the last eight cars stood precariously at the edge of the mountain jutting into the void, the rest of the Transcontinental Express plunged into the jaws of the mountains. It burst into flames, the falling bits and pieces of the Grubenmanns' timber feeding the raging fire.

There was a tremendous explosion, then complete, macabre silence. Little remained as wreckage. Twisted steel. A shoe. A stethoscope. Catherine's soap-bubble ring. One of Kaplan's shiny watches, charred.

Of the eight salvaged cars, three – the security and supplies – were entirely empty.

Jennifer, Ginger, Parsons, Tom and the other survivors, including Catherine, stared out through the gaping hole where the train had broken off. They looked into the smoking ruins below. They were still.

Somewhere a telephone was ringing.

26 5.16pm

Mackenzie lifted the receiver. The flashing red light on the wall screen map died on his face and went out.

'I see,' he said impassively. 'Thank you.'

He hung up. He turned around to the others, avoiding Elena's eyes.

'Milestone was conceived in secrecy,' he said. 'It will remain in secrecy.'

He moved to the tape that had recorded all that had transpired at the Milestone Command Centre. The reels continued to turn. He reached for the 'Destruct' button.

Elena stopped him, holding his arm. He looked at her. His eyes were inscrutable. The doors opened. A voice bellowed.

'We cannot oppose the will of the governments!'

It was Hoffmann. Mackenzie did not move. He could feel the warmth of Elena's hand gripping his arm.

'We can try!' Elena pleaded with Mackenzie. Hers were the last words on the tape.

Mackenzie stared at Elena for a moment. He searched her eyes seeking strength. But he could not find it. He could look at her no longer. He cast his eyes downward.

He pressed 'Destruct' – as if he were destroying himself. The reels began to spin. A high-frequency hum grew to piercing intensity. Elena's hand shot up to cover her ears. She turned the injured one away, driving her palms against the sides of her head.

*

Jennifer, Parsons and Tom were helping the surviving passengers jump two or three feet from the detached part of the train to the ground. Ginger was with Catherine. Susan and Betty cared for the baby. The sun was going down, a disc of blood that had splattered the hazy sky.

They were all being watched on a line that ran along the top of the barrel of a gun.

Blood dripping from a wound in his shoulder, staining his stark white clothing, a guard was approaching. Suddenly, Catherine saw him. She tugged at Jennifer, who turned and stood face to face with their pursuer, a face hidden by its immaculate white mask. Jennifer called to him in a voice broken with emotion.

'Who are you?'

There was no answer. He seemed unsteady on his feet.

'I must know who you are!' she cried rushing to him with open hands.

Parsons tried to stop her as she ran past him, but she spun away from him and continued.

The guard fired. The bullet ripped away her camera. She looked in horror. The entire record had been destroyed. Her fury mounted. She charged the guard shouting wildly.

'Take off your mask!'

Her hands came down like bestial claws tearing away the covering on his face. He fought her. A shot rang out. The guard's mask remained clutched in Jennifer's hand as he sank to the ground. He was dead.

She stared into the revealed face: a handsome young man no more than twenty-two years old. Jennifer was unbeliev-

ing. She had expected a monster and had found only a helpless creature like herself.

She turned in the direction from where the bullet had
come. Chamberlain, a battered man, but wearing the pain of
the living, stood not ten yards away. She squinted at him in
disbelief. She turned to the others. They smiled joyously.

She began to hurry to him. He grinned broadly. He
tried to run to her, but his leg wound reduced his pace to
a painful hobble. Yet he continued.

Jennifer, beaming, cried to him at the top of her lungs.

'Sonofabitch!' she shouted. Then she cupped her hands
around her mouth. 'WHICH PHONE BOOK?'

Her hair streaming, she raced towards him like the wind.

Epilogue

Stephen Mackenzie resigned four hours after the Transcontinental Express went down, Elena Lindstrom on the following day. Mackenzie was retired on full pension. He withdrew to his farm near the medieval Tuscan village of Pieve a Presciano, where he produced high-quality olive oil, Chianti wine and an occasional paper (usually of a cautionary nature) on the problems of the new science of ecological epidemiology. Elena has returned to her native Sweden, where she is currently engaged in research she defines as being 'less ambitious than before'.

Gregorovius Hoffmann was appointed acting director of the Milestone project, filling Mackenzie's post. From the point of view of 'the will of the governments' he did an admirable job in covering up what was thereafter referred to officially as 'the Grubenmann incident'. His principal tasks, apart from the cover-up, were a thorough compilation of a report on the 'incident', the liquidation of the Milestone papers (ultimately to include his own report), and the dismantling of the project itself. Here he succeeded again, and when Milestone was disbanded, his diligence earned him an even higher position with his own government – in the Ministry of Defence, as head of the cryptic Ausserordentlich Forschungbüro, or the Office of Extraordinary Research.

As for his report and the Milestone papers, bureaucracy being what it is, it was decided – through no lapse on Hoffmann's part – merely to classify rather than physically destroy them, a decision which has since led to their disclosure in a most unofficial way. I have a copy of the Hoffmann report. Written in his unmistakable style, it contains the following sentence:

'Of the 1,237 persons positively identified as subjects of the incident, i.e. the total number of passengers, crew, and other personnel, no less than 1,140 were aboard the section of the train which was unsuccessful in negotiating the so-called Cassandra Crossing; of these, all, of course, were non-survivors.'

Ostensibly this means that there were ninety-seven persons who were not 'non-survivors', or in less involuted language, they lived. This is not entirely true.

From the ninety-seven, one must subtract Kaplan, whose remains, incidentally, were never found, and the guard whom Chamberlain was forced to kill in defence of Jennifer's life. Also, on the salvaged part of the train were the bodies of two guards, Mrs Chadwick, the 'priest', and the mother of the sick baby.

Of the ninety actual survivors, only eighty-four were passengers, the rest being part of the medical team which boarded at Kleve and whose only function seems to have been the entombment of persons killed not by the disease but by gunfire.

The fate of the surviving passengers has more or less been learned. Held by the local authorities at the site of the Cassandra Crossing, they were flown to the 'health camp' at Janow Station and kept in quarantine and incommunicado – not for twenty-one but forty-five days, the additional period being considered necessary, it seems, for the cover-up operation. None of them took ill from the disease, although two elderly persons are said to have died of 'natural causes', which is certainly misleading because it does not take into account the hardship they suffered, undoubtedly hastening their death.

Much of the period of quarantine was spent in an attempt to indoctrinate the survivors with questionable reasoning as to why they should participate in withholding from friends, relatives and the press the true fate of the Transcontinental Express (to prevent worldwide panic, protect international security, etc). Obviously, it was known that this effort could not be one hundred per cent effective, particularly since

Chamberlain and his group signed a statement of protest in which they announced their intention 'to inform the world'. But, according to the Hoffmann report, the brain-washing operation was designed to disorient the survivors (Hoffmann calls it 'preventive orientation') so that whatever stories got out from some, contradictions would emerge from others.

Indeed, when the survivors were released, only a handful tried to tell of their experience, and while it made local news in various parts of the world, little further attention was aroused and the affair was quickly forgotten much in the manner of UFO sightings. My own experience in attempting to interview, and in a few cases succeeding, some of these survivors revealed a great reluctance to speak about the 'incident', and when they did the facts were invariably scrambled and confused.

The only independent eyewitness to the collapse of the Cassandra Crossing was Jan Cieszyn, the shepherd. He reported what he had seen to the Ostrava police in precise detail. The factual part of his story that was made public, along with the discrediting additional material, may be seen in the news dispatch reprinted at the beginning of this book. Following his release after several days of questioning and detention, Cieszyn never again spoke of the matter, nor of what took place during his highly irregular incarceration.

It is to the credit of Jonathan Chamberlain that he foresaw all this and that he waited for the initial interest in the case – however slight – to subside. He used the time to reflect, recall and reconstruct, and to seek what he felt was the best way in which the full story might be told. To accomplish this, he took an extended vacation in a most remote and tranquil place, an adobe ruin of a house he owned in New Mexico. As might be expected, he was accompanied by Jennifer Saint.

Not very long ago, I received a cable from Jennifer inviting me to Placitas – no ticket, no explanation, just an invitation. Because it was Jennifer, I went. I worked for a month helping Chamberlain restore his house. He taught me how to mix cement, carry wooden beams and lift adobe blocks. I never saw a more contented man than he. I had never known Jennifer so capable of happiness. I had never seen two people so much in love.

While we worked we talked – which is how this book came to be written.

Postscript

As these pages go to press, one nagging question remains. The disease that took lodging on the Transcontinental Express did not die with the Cassandra Crossing. Only a singular genetic variant was vanquished by a singular circumstance. The threat foreseen by Langer and Bernstein is still with us, intensifying, and all the good and not-so-good intentions that created Milestone flourish, too. Can it happen all over again – if not in the same, in some other way?

I recently revisited Duke Mackenzie. He was anticipating the arrival that afternoon of his daughter, Melanie, and he seemed in rare form. We walked under a dazzling sun among his well-kept vines. The *Sangiovese*, *Malvasia* and *Trebbiano* grapes pendulated in an afternoon wind. I asked him my question. He thought a while, weighed a *grappolo* in his palm, and plucked and ate a *Malvasia*, seeds and all. He said something about the sugar content being nice and high and that picking time was coming on, though he hoped he could wait for one more rain, and a final burst of sunshine; and then he answered.

'If it can,' he said with a rural attenuation of his words, 'it will.'

Other Pan books that may interest you
are listed on the following pages

Hopscotch 60p
Brian Garfield

From the author of *Kolchak's Gold*

Miles Kendig was the best field man in the CIA. Now he's too old and he's too hot — and he's out. But Kendig still has a trick or two up his ex-Agency sleeve . . .

Threatening global publication of stories that the world's cloak-and-dagger men hardly dare tell each other, he sets himself up as the quarry in a nailbiting international manhunt.

'Brian Garfield knows how to turn the excitement up to full pitch' EVENING STANDARD

Extreme Remedies 75p
John Hejinian

Surgeons performing experimental operations on unsuspecting victims . . . Organ transplanters moving in like vultures on comatose patients . . . Nurses feeding their own addictions with stolen drugs . . . Human life being treated with inhuman indifference, every day of the year.

'The best doctor-patient-hospital book, fiction or non-fiction, that I have read in years . . . a first-rate suspense story' NEW YORK TIMES

Marathon Man 70p
William Goldman

By the author of *Butch Cassidy and the Sundance Kid*

'The best American thriller this year . . . you won't put this one down' WASHINGTON POST

Stumbling into the violent world of couriers and assassins, knives and Magnum force guns, espionage and torture, the boy who dreamed of winning races suddenly becomes a man running for his life . . .

'Keeps you on the edge of your seat with that combination of terror and pleasure only the superb thriller can achieve' LIBRARY JOURNAL

Now a successful film starring Dustin Hoffman and Laurence Olivier

Arthur Hailey

Record-breaking bestsellers from the acclaimed master of blockbusting epic fiction

The Final Diagnosis 80p

The enthralling story of a young pathologist and his efforts to restore the standards of a hospital controlled by an ageing, once brilliant doctor. One faulty diagnosis — one irrevocable error — precipitates tragedy. The intrigues, heartbreaks and triumphs of a world no patient sees are brilliantly explored.

Flight Into Danger 80p

As the airliner droned westwards through the Canadian night, the fierce, unheralded terror struck. The peaceful, happy evening became a hideous nightmare. And hundreds of miles away, on solid ground at Vancouver Airport, everyone watched and prayed. Silent. Helpless . . .

Airport 80p

Nonstop reading excitement as Arthur Hailey probes the hidden nerve-centre that controls a great modern airport.
'Supercharged' CHICAGO SUN-TIMES

Hotel 75p

The scene is the St Gregory Hotel, New Orleans. Through this totally fascinating novel move vividly drawn characters. And there are robbery and blackmail, a near-disastrous orgy and a take-over battle . . . courage too, and a love story that will remain etched on the reader's mind.

Gavin Lyall
Blame the Dead 60p

'Superior, tough yet pensive thriller, full of twists and turns from Harrow schoolboys to Norwegian alcoholics' OBSERVER

Judas Country 70p

'Skilful mixture of ageing flyers, with planes to match, battling their way through arms smuggling, Middle East intrigue and the tale of a fabulous sword which once belonged to Richard the Lion-heart . . . Must be contender for the best crime book of the year' DAILY MIRROR

Midnight Plus One 70p

'Motor dash from Brittany to Austrian border; cars crumple, bullets fly . . . a magnificent cliffhanger' SATURDAY REVIEW

The Most Dangerous Game 70p

'Gavin Lyall writes with zest and bite repeating, and splendidly, his triumph in *The Wrong Side of the Sky*' NEW YORK TIMES

Shooting Script 60p

'The vortex of Caribbean politics made even more turbulent . . . by one of the most compelling of contemporary storytellers' NEW YORK TIMES

Venus With Pistol 60p

'Works up to beautiful tension and ingenuity in Vienna – via London, Amsterdam, Zurich and Venice' TIMES LITERARY SUPPLEMENT

Selected bestsellers

☐ **The Eagle Has Landed** Jack Higgins 80p
☐ **The Moneychangers** Arthur Hailey 95p
☐ **Marathon Man** William Goldman 70p
☐ **Nightwork** Irwin Shaw 75p
☐ **Tropic of Ruislip** Leslie Thomas 75p
☐ **One Flew Over The Cuckoo's Nest** Ken Kesey 75p
☐ **Collision** Spencer Dunmore 70p
☐ **Perdita's Prince** Jean Plaidy 70p
☐ **The Eye of the Tiger** Wilbur Smith 80p
☐ **The Shootist** Glendon Swarthout 60p
☐ **Of Human Bondage** Somerset Maugham 95p
☐ **Rebecca** Daphne du Maurier 80p
☐ **Slay Ride** Dick Francis 60p
☐ **Jaws** Peter Benchley 70p
☐ **Let Sleeping Vets Lie** James Herriot 60p
☐ **If Only They Could Talk** James Herriot 60p
☐ **It Shouldn't Happen to a Vet** James Herriot 60p
☐ **Vet In Harness** James Herriot 60p
☐ **Tinker Tailor Soldier Spy** John le Carré 75p
☐ **Gone with the Wind** Margaret Mitchell £1.75
☐ **Cashelmara** Susan Howatch £1.25
☐ **The Nonesuch** Georgette Heyer 60p
☐ **The Grapes of Wrath** John Steinbeck 95p
☐ **Drum** Kyle Onstott 60p

All these books are available at your bookshop or newsagent;
or can be obtained direct from the publisher
Pan Books, Cavaye Place, London SW10 9PG

Just tick the titles you want and fill in the form below

Prices quoted are applicable in UK

Send purchase price plus 15p for the first book and 5p for each
additional book, to allow for postage and packing

Name _____
(block letters please)
Address _____

_____

While every effort is made to keep prices low, it is sometimes
necessary to increase prices at short notice. Pan Books reserve the
right to show on covers new retail prices which may differ from
those advertised in the text or elsewhere